The Breath of God

Shannon Renner

DORRANCE PUBLISHING CO
EST. 1920
PITTSBURGH, PENNSYLVANIA 15238

The contents of this work, including, but not limited to, the accuracy of events, people, and places depicted; opinions expressed; permission to use previously published materials included; and any advice given or actions advocated are solely the responsibility of the author, who assumes all liability for said work and indemnifies the publisher against any claims stemming from publication of the work.

All Rights Reserved
Copyright © 2022 by Shannon Renner

No part of this book may be reproduced or transmitted, downloaded, distributed, reverse engineered, or stored in or introduced into any information storage and retrieval system, in any form or by any means, including photocopying and recording, whether electronic or mechanical, now known or hereinafter invented without permission in writing from the publisher.

Dorrance Publishing Co
585 Alpha Drive
Suite 103
Pittsburgh, PA 15238
Visit our website at *www.dorrancebookstore.com*

ISBN: 978-1-6853-7125-8
eISBN: 978-1-6853-7970-4

Prologue: Seven Years After 'The Day the Earth Shook'

It is up to you, the reader of my journal, to decide if what they did was right or if their quest to better the human race was their undoing. I, of all, people cannot be the judge of that.

BOOM BOOM BOOM.

Oh my God, that sound is driving me nuts. The vibrations were becoming very unnerving and the cacophony of sounds grated on us like fingernails on a chalkboard. The pounding coming from Top Side is getting closer, louder, and more frightening every day. What started over a year ago as a distant tapping, like a drip from a water pipe far off in the walls, has slowly turned into the unmistakable sounds of someone or something clawing its way down to us. I am told it is the sound of heavy industrial equipment. I have no idea what industrial equipment sounds like, and with all communications severed, I cannot look it up online. I just have to take their word for it. Obviously, I rely way too much on the Internet. Why did I spend my spare time watching old movies instead of researching industrial equipment? Really!? Because I was fifteen when we lost connection, that's why. And there was no way I could have known the information would be imperative seven years in the future, so sue me. As far as I know, I was a typical teenager. Wow, was I wrong, in ways I would never have believed.

We surely only have a matter of weeks before our barriers are breached. I have decided to begin a journal of what happened to us, to the world, or at least as much as I know and can put down on paper before whatever or whoever reaches us. Don't take my writing as gospel truth. I am no historian; in fact, I am twenty-two years old and have spent my entire life here in New Eden. I was born here. I am the only one here that has never been to the surface. What my journal will tell is my experiences and what I have read or been told. Please excuse my mistakes and lack of artistic talent. If you don't like it, well my friend, don't bother to read it. Easy peasy lemon squeezy.

BOOM BOOM

I do not know how long it has taken them to locate us or dig through the mile of dirt and clay to reach our outer wall. We have no way of knowing their intentions once our ten-foot steel walls are compromised or what sort of contaminants will flood our environment, if any. So, in short, we know nothing and imagine the worst. People are acting crazy now, and I dare to imagine how we will all handle the truth, whatever it ends up being.

BOOM BOOM BOOM

It is difficult to ignore the sounds of the intruders. Especially since it only happens at night. Top Side was wiped out nearly seven years ago on my fifteenth birthday so, Happy Birthday to me. I hope you get the sarcasm. Those of us here in the fortress of New Eden were unaffected by whatever happened up there. In fact, we have no clue what really did happen. Only theories, speculations, and fears have run wild over the years. Lately, since the obvious excavation began, those theories have multiplied and become the subject of sheer panic.

On that day, seven years ago, The Day the Earth Shook, as we have come to call it, all of the monitors and signals of any kind from Top Side disappeared. There has been no communication from anyone anywhere since that day. Trust me, in all of this time, we have tried everything that the greatest minds of our collective could think of to do. Literally, we have the greatest minds on Earth down here. In fact, that is why they are down here. This was to be their salvation and refuge to work on the world's problems. The ultimate think tank and laboratory for the world's greatest minds. Has it turned into a deadly trap? Would we all have been better off on the surface at the time of, well, the time of whatever happened? I guess we will soon find out.

BOOM

We are all scared. The possibilities of what lies ahead are endless. Will we be saved from isolation? Will we be contaminated by radiation or viruses, or will our existence as we know it to be raped and pillaged? For sure, we will know the answer sooner than we want to. I am ashamed to admit that I am actually kind of excited. I feel an adventure coming. I have never been on the surface. My life has been very limited, experience-wise, and I have always felt that I have been treated differently than everyone else, almost like an outsider in my own skin. I need answers that no one here will provide. Maybe those answers are coming. What I have learned since this began is: love is a breath away from hate, lost is so close to found, and there is no difference between a saint and a sinner other than perception and timing.

Chapter One: My Family

I presume the first thing I should do is introduce myself. My name is Enola Evangeline O'Ceallaigh. I am the only child of Merrin Deniege Mackenzie and Jean Baptiste Deklin O'Ceallaigh. They both are Pulitzer Prize winning scientists from Ireland. My parents worked here in New Ede , the city located a mile beneath the Earth's surface. I have not seen or heard from them since my fifteenth birthday. I know in my heart that they must be dead, but I hope that they somehow are living somewhere underground as I am. I cling to that and look forward to being with them again.

My mother, let's see, how should I describe her? She is short of stature with a bone structure that models would kill for and long silky-smooth blond hair always worn in a braid that hung past her thin waist. Though only five foot five, her muscular legs and athletic build make her appear lanky. She has a way a moving like liquid, floating through a room with purpose. She is a platinum blonde with the bluest eyes I've ever seen and skin as pale as cotton. Did I mention that she is stubborn as a rock? If you had met her for only a few moments, I would not have to mention it. Born and raised in Galway, Ireland, she completed all of her studies there with her parents who were scientists also. They never made it to the United States. Unfortunately, they were killed by a car bomb. It wasn't even in their car but rather the car parked next to them in traffic. This all occurred when my mother was just starting college. She inherited their apartment, money, and drive to change the world.

My mother dedicated her every minute to study and research. I was told she never dated or even had friends after my grandparents' death. She had become determined to use her skills to make sure the violence of society ended. They were a well-off family with copious connections in politics. As high society as one gets in Galway. Their apartment was two thousand square feet and furnished with all the latest electronics. No paintings or antiques not even a family portrait decorated it. There was a library and a home lab. My mother never had a chance of being anything but an intellectual. My grandparents would never have allowed it. My mother was homeschooled until college. Their home was more scientific research center than anything else. No wonder she was so at ease in New Eden.

When she obtained her master's degree in Genetic Development and Theory, she immigrated to the United States of America. She arrived with nothing but a suitcase of clothes that were very appropriate for the climate in Colorado and several crates of her own research. There she worked in a kind of think tank, where eleven other top-rated scientists studied the changes going on throughout the planet. That is where she met my good old dad. From the moment she burst into the laboratory she was assigned to, she took it over. She has that way about her. She was like a leprechaun that struts in and is instantly the center of attention and commands respect. Her mere presence was enough to put most men in awe. Her flippant attitude made them all try in vain to get her attention. She only had eyes for the lab work and my father. In that order.

My father is tall, and he seemed like a giant to me as a child. His hair is as orange as the flames in the fireplace. His eyes as green as jade that always had a wink for me when our eyes met. He has always been painfully shy and reserved. How my parents got together and blended so well is beyond me. He was also born, raised, and studied in Ireland. Unlike my city girl mother, he was from a very small farming community called Saint Helene. His parents owned and worked a sheep farm on several hundred acres of beautiful rolling green hills that stretched all the way to the crashing ocean waves upon the bright red cliffs. I have seen the pictures. He grew up having to get his education bit by bit. His professors recognized his extraordinary talent with the land and new innovative ways of growing crops and keeping the livestock free from diseases that were plaguing the area. He was given a full scholarship and excelled beyond their expectations.

While away at university, his parents were killed during a raid on their underground church. Religion was outlawed by then. The Catholics in their town all met in a storm cellar to practice their beliefs. One of their parishioners was caught with a rosary in town by an informant. The soldiers held her children hostage, raping and beating them until she gave up the church's location. They located the storm cellar and boarded the door shut. Church was in session and no one heard them arrive. Everyone was burned alive in the cellar, then the soldiers returned to the home of the tortured woman and did the same to her and her family.

After his family's untimely death, my father moved to the United States of America to work for the same think tank my mother had been recruited by. He sold the farm and all of the livestock to his cousin to purchase his way. He had no other relatives and never had the charisma or desire to make friends. He packed up his few things and his genetic engineering degree and never looked back.

For my parents, it was love at first accent. They reminded each other of home and all of the things they missed. Their backgrounds were so similar and having both lost their parents to the raging civil conflicts cemented a bond between them. I always loved watching my parents together. They couldn't walk past one another without touching and looking into each other's eyes. Their love, respect, and dedication to one another just radiated from them like an aurora. I know is sounds as if I am romanticizing it all, and I probably am a little. But this is my view of my parents.

I was born in Under Earth, Fortress 7, District 32, facility 27, which is located on the continent of North America, directly under the Denver Airport in the area formerly known as Colorado. I am the only child who was ever born here and the only person here that has never been to Top Side. I am told that there are a few like me in other Fortresses, but we are few. I inherited my father's hair, but mine seems to never do what I want it to. It is long, curly, and a deep shade of red with peach highlights, a shade I have never seen on anyone else. My skin, having never been exposed to the sun, is very pale, almost translucent. It always has a light sheen to it, as if I constantly apply moisturizer. It reminds me of salamander skin. My best friend is jealous of my skin, and the fact that the only place I have hair on my body is my head. Again, I am told it is because I have never been exposed to a natural environment. I have eyes like no one else I have ever met also. My father has remarkable green eyes and my mother's eyes are a striking blue.

My eyes are truly purple with clear irises that are shaped like a thin oval stretched up and down, sort of goat-like. I never noticed how odd that was until one day when an older child I was playing with pointed it out to me. My parents told me it was a genetic family trait that skips a generation and the other child had never seen anyone else with it. I am short, but taller than my mom by half an inch. I also did not inherit my mother's curves. Don't get me wrong, it is obvious I am a girl, but I am not what you would call sexy. I fear that both my parents kept their intellect to themselves. I mean, I am not saying I am a retard or anything, I just don't have the drive they seem to possess when it comes to science and math, okay, well in school in general. It all seems so pointless. Why relearn what I already know? Why study what has already been studied or has already happened? I guess my mind just does not work like theirs.

My best friend Zeynep Bhourdi is of course a Top Side baby. She is six years older than I and the polar opposite of me. She is unpredictable and constantly in motion, like a fire running wild. She blazes through everything and everyone. She is tall, five feet ten inches with short cropped hair as black as coal, blue eyes, and olive skin. She has traveled around the world with her parents. They are researchers and scientists working on DNA. She was born in India, but just like me, her parents were brilliant scientist who took positions at a think tank. Zeynep, or Z as we call her, arrived in Under Earth when I was four and she was ten. Already she was taller than some of the adults. I remember that day like it was yesterday. She entered my life like a storm and has not stopped moving since. She was allowed to go to Top Side with her parents until she was old enough to stay down here by herself. Well, not really by herself. She was with me and my nanny. Of course, she goes up anyway whenever she pleases. She is not much for rules and as far as I know, she has never been caught.

Although, she does put strict rules on me and even reprimands adults when they don't treat me as she thinks they should. What can I say? I am special to her. She finds our life here boring, and being the free spirit she is, no one can stop her. It is one of the reasons I love her so much and also one of the reasons she drives me crazy. I guess that is what best friends are for. There is no one else here close to our age. The closest is Shane, who was five years older than Z and kind of a bad boy. He was beautiful in a dark way. Thick black hair dark eyes and mocha skin. He was always in trouble, carried a knife with him everywhere, and I swear I saw him smoking a cigarette a few times. We watched him from a distance, like a game. He is the Big Bad Wolf and we are the curious little pigs with a crush.

I have never been to Top Side, though my parents worked there and traveled back and forth a couple times a month. They did not want me exposed to the brutality, disease, and dangers that were every day occurrences there. I have seen Top Side on the computer monitors in the main control room. I have watched every movie I could download to my personal chip and endlessly questioned everyone I know who has been there. I love old movies, even the ones that don't have color or even sound. They show me a world I do not know and never will know and the adventures I will never have. We have animals and plants here, but I have never felt a breeze, seen the moon and stars, or felt the warmth of the sun on my skin. These may seem like trivial things to someone who has experienced those luxuries their entire lives. To me, those are the things of my dreams. Experiences I always hoped I would have, like holding hands with a boy. Now it is all gone. I will never get the chance to smell the ocean, swim in salty water filled with marine life, or climb a willow tree. Oh, how I would love to see birds in flight, a falling star, or even bugs. Yes, bugs. I have never seen one. I know, stop whining and get on with the story.

Chapter Two: The Day the Earth Shook

Almost seven years ago…

"Get up, you lazy bump!" I had my pillow over my face, but I knew the voice of my best friend. "Ugh, it is early you know," I whined through the three hundred count linen pillowcase. I moved the pillow and turned toward the sounds of her foot impatiently tapping. Z was leaning against the door jamb of my bedroom, arms and legs crossed, and looking very displeased with me. "Okay, okay," I grumbled while very ungracefully stumbling out of bed toward the bathroom. "Just give me five minutes and I will be ready to go." Z walked, well, no, she never just walked, she sashayed over to my closet and began sorting out what she wanted me to wear to the mall.

"You know, Enola, if we do not hurry we will be late. I told you I would be here at ten and your lazy ass is still in bed. It is your birthday for Christ's sake, and I have plans for you so hurry up. Ah! Just the outfit." I peek out of the bathroom, toothpaste dripping from my lip, and see her holding up the skimpiest thing she could have possibly found in my closet. " Is that even mine?" I sighed through my toothbrush. Z giggled, "Actually it used to be mine, remember I gave it to you like two years ago, and you still haven't worn it? Now come on, do I have to get your underthings ready for you too?"

I quickly ran my hands through my unruly curls and twisted my hair into a high ponytail. I made a huge deal out of putting on the barely-there clothes she chose for me and sat at my vanity so she could do my makeup. I swear she acted like I was a doll to dress and play with instead of her best friend. It did me no good to argue, so I just gave in and let her have her way. "Why were you still in bed?" she badgered me. "Well, I found some interesting reading on the computer last night, and by the time I looked at the clock, it was 4:00 A.M." "Let me guess," she smirked, "you were studying up on genetic research again?" She rolled her eyes as I nodded and resumed with the plastering of my face. I can't help it! Once I discovered that not too long before the Fortresses were built, people who could afford it had their children engineered. They would go to a lab and pick out every detail about their child from a list: eye color, hair color, skin color, propensity for sports or math. The list goes on and on and on.

The price of this was incredibly high and depended on how specific you wanted to get. How weird. It really just takes nature, God, chance whatever out of it. Who would want that? I admit taking defects or disease out is great, but programming their likes and dislikes is crazy. People had to have a legal permit to have a child and those found pregnant without one were executed. They did not want the poor, uneducated, or genetically inferior to procreate. A part of me gets that line of thinking, I mean with all of the overpopulation, poverty, and disease who would want to bring a child into that?

Z's personality is much more aggressive than mine. I am stubborn and sarcastic, believe me, but having lived my life in Under Earth with not many people to spend time with, my social skills and experiences are limited. Z has been to Top Side and has a boyfriend named Eban who lives up there. She has a few times tried to sneak him down here but has yet to be successful with that. She was even born up there and only moved here when she was ten. She goes up once a week and meets Eban for their date. When she gets back she tells me all about what they did, well not everything. She thankfully leaves out all the sex. The first time she started to tell me about it I got so embarrassed I ran out of the room, so she leaves that part out now.

Now that my makeup was complete, off we went to start my birthday celebration together. Finally, fifteen, the age when I get to start college and work in the lab. That is how our morning started on the last day or the first day, however, you want to look at it. It was the last day of the lives we knew. The last day of normalcy and dreaming of futures we would never get to experience. It was the first day of a new reality one we could never have dreamed of or wished for. We had no clue what the day would bring. Z planned for us to spend the day at the mall. The movie theatre was featuring the movie marathon of my dreams, the all-time best movies of the 20th century. I'd seen them all several times of course, but I really loved them.

We exited the residential facilities and walked to the tram system, arm in arm, chatting and giggling as we climbed into the railcar. I sucked in my breath as the doors shut, as I always did. I hate tram cars with a passion. Maybe I am claustrophobic, maybe I just don't like being this close to this many people, whatever the issue is, it freaks me out. Immediately, Z squeezed me tightly and said, "It will just take ten minutes. You know this. I've got you, so just breathe and concentrate on the lady two rows up with the crazy-ass green hair." It was Juniper Lee! She and her twin sister Juneau are the seamstresses who make all of the clothes, linens, etc.

We both started to giggle again as soon as she said that, which made the ride seem to go by fast and eased my anxieties. The car doors slid open with that awful sucking noise they make, and we exited as quickly as possible.

The two of us just about ran down the corridor trying to beat all the commuters to the main area of our facility which contained the mall, greenhouse, agricultural centers, labs, water renewal systems, energy conservation center, and supply warehousing. Most people were off to work while we were off to spend our day eating junk food and frying our brains on movies. That is when the security doors between the hub and the tram system, the ones we had just walked through not three seconds ago, slammed shut, shaking the entire facility and making a crashing sound loud enough to make us all deaf. Those of us close to the doors were thrown to the ground. Z and I lie sprawled out, face first in a daze.

We both turned to look at each other and the expression on my face must surely have resembled the look on hers. She was scared and confused and about to panic. I reached out my hand to her, and we grabbed on to each other and tried to help each other up. The ringing in my ears was so loud I could not make out what she was saying, I could see her lips moving, but my eyes were blurry and my ears felt like they may be bleeding. Before we could stand, the entire facility began to shake, slowly at first and then it gradually got stronger and more powerful. We stayed on the ground, clutching each other, and crying. It seemed to last forever, but it was only about five minutes. Once it finally stopped, we were all able to get up, brush ourselves off, and then everyone started talking at once. A few minutes later, the world started to shake again, just not with the same intensity as before and not as long. It did that several times before it stopped for good.

This entire scene reminded me of when the Wicked Witch of the East wrote "surrender Dorothy" in the sky of Oz and all the people huddled together chattering about what to do. Then, they decided to go see The Wizard, he would know what to do. Well, we don't have a wizard but we do have a control center that houses hundreds of Top Side cameras and communications systems all over the world. Most people headed to the Control Center. Those who were injured headed to the medical facility, and those who were not interested in the scientific mumbo jumbo that was being chatted about headed to get a drink and settle themselves. Z grabbed me by my hand, "Come on, let's go get a seat in the cafe. If we wait too long, there will be too many people in there. No one is in a hurry to get to work until they figure out what happened and get the doors back up." "The doors are only supposed to close if our facility or one of the connecting facilities is under attack," I whispered.

"There must have been an earthquake or something," Z assured me. We slid into a corner booth and began to examine each other for any injuries. Neither of us had anything more than a few scrapes and bruises. We ordered some sparkling juice and settled back in our seats, listening to the people at the tables around us discussing the event. Everyone had their own theories as to what we all just experienced, from earthquakes to an alien invasion. There had never been an earthquake in this area in the entire recorded history of earthquakes but strange shit happens all the time. There were no more militaries, so that rules out some kind of war. Mrs. Bryant, head of the accounting division, who was our resident religious freak, thought it was the end of the world. She was at the next table with Father Joe, of course, and three ladies who worked in the mall, all of whom Z swears have a huge crush on Father Joe. Why wouldn't they? He is very handsome, intelligent, and so kind all the time. Well, he is kind to everyone but me. He avoids contact with me when he can. Don't get me wrong, he is never rude. I think maybe it is my eyes. He never makes eye contact with me. He has never tried to talk religion with me either. Things that make you go hmmm.

"Armageddon!" shouted Mrs. Bryant. "Mark my words, I tell you, the Lord has come for us all. The rapture has taken place." I was facing the back of Father Joe's head, but I knew he rolled his eyes. For a priest, he was really cool. Well, to be honest, he is the only priest I have ever met, but from what I've heard from other people and seen on T.V., most priests acted more like Mrs. Bryant. Father Joe lifted his hands is a gesture of bewilderment, looked at Mrs. Bryant, and stated, "And you would think that a woman of your faith would have joined Christ in his Father's Holy Kingdom, but alas, it appears you are still here with us, my dear."

We could hardly suppress the laughter at the look on Mrs. Bryant's face. She was desperately trying to speak but the words just came out all jumbled, half-spoken, ill-formed, and lost on her tongue. She finally spurted out, "Well it could not have been the Rapture then. I hadn't thought about none of us disappearing, I was just confused. It has been a very shocking day, don't you agree?" "Yes," interjected Hannah, who worked at the book store in the mall. "It has been a fucked-up morning for sure. Oh, sorry Father, it just kind of slipped out." Hannah had her hand over her mouth and her cheeks were flushed with embarrassment. Father Joe gently removed her hand from her face as he gave it a little squeeze, "How many times do I have to tell you girls that I am not the vocabulary police? Be yourself, no commandment says you can't utilize expletives. Just don't take the Lord's name in vain. You should hear what escapes my lips when I hit my thumb with a hammer. God is not monitoring the little shit."

You could visibly see all four ladies at his table sigh and melt as they stared at him like lost puppies. We could not help ourselves. We starting laughing so hard that we spilled our drinks and knocked the salt shaker off of our table. We couldn't stop. I know, it was crazy, but we just lost it. I think it was the built-up tension and fear from the event that would soon become known as "The Day the Earth Shook".

That is what we all started referring to it as, and it stuck. Everyone in the cafe turned to watch us as we laughed so hard we were crying. It took a few minutes to get ourselves together and realize that we had become the center of attention. Father Joe looked concerned, "You girls okay?" We both started mumbling something about everything being fine, but we were embarrassed and a little scared too. Sharri, a hefty Scottish woman who is in charge of the animals at the Agricultural Center, said, "That's one way to let it out. The healthy way for sure. You guys go ahead and laugh all you want. It's better than hearing about the Rapture any day."

We were all hanging out at the cafe and court area of the mall when the group of people who went to the Control Center returned. By the looks on their faces, we knew that the news was not going to be good. There was probably close to a hundred and fifty of us there that day, gathered in the court waiting to hear what the others had found out from Control Center. It was suddenly very quiet. Someone had even silenced the mall background music. I never noticed it was not playing its usual tunes until this very minute when everyone was quiet. No one was talking, there was no shuffling of feet scraping of chairs, just complete silence. The silence gave the moment an ominous effect. It felt as if maybe they were going to tell us that it was the end of the world, and we had been forgotten about down here. I grabbed Z's hand and held it tightly as Dr. Pratte began to speak. Dr. Pratte was head of the research department in the lab. He stepped up onto the center court stage where we held concerts on Friday nights. He walked to the edge facing the crowd and cleared his throat. He looked out of place on stage and unaccustomed to public speaking.

"Can everyone hear me?" he began. He paused for a moment looking over the crowd before continuing. "There was not a large amount of information available to us. All of the Top Side monitors have been disabled. All communication systems with Top Side and the other Facilities has been compromised also." With that, the crowd began asking questions all at once. "What happened up there?" some screamed. Most were asking what we were going to do. Dr. Pratte raised his hands up to calm the crowd and get them to listen to what he had to say. "Let me finish, please. We were able to roll back the recorded data on the computer from before the earth shook. Everything looks as it should, there was nothing out of the ordinary. Then suddenly, there was some kind of electromagnetic disturbance everywhere. The monitors wavered a bit. Areas that had people in view showed them all stop and look around as if there was something amiss. Some people started running while others huddled together and some seemed not really to notice. Then… Then, well it is hard to explain, but you can all watch it for yourselves."

Dr. Pratte went on, "The best I can explain is that there came a visible breeze that seemed to slowly destroy everything it touched. As it hit the monitors, we lost visual, it took a few more seconds to lose audio. That was the worst part. The sounds were a mixture of screams grinding metal and wind." Dr. Pratte just shook his head and ran his hand down his face, visibly shaken. "Let me suggest that everyone keep up with their assigned duties. We need to get a list going of who is here and who is not. We will assign appropriate people to take over the jobs of those who are missing. We will immediately start checking all of our feeds from the surface for power, water, and air. As you know, our facilities can produce everything we need ,should we be entirely cut off. We have enough supplies of things not produced here to get us through years, and none of those items are truly essential to life anyway." Dr. Pratte seemed to scan the crowd and stopped as we made eye contact. He suddenly smiled, gave a little nod, then walked off stage toward the labs.

Did you see that? Dr. Pratte seemed to look for me and was happy I was here. What is that all about? Z just shrugged her shoulders, grabbed my hand, and hustled me through the crowd. She did not say a word until we were out of the courtyard and in the hall that leads to the theatre. "I hope the movies are still on for today. No need to drop our birthday plans just because of some electronic weirdness at Top Side." I stopped in my tracks, pulled my hand from hers, and said, "Really? You want to go to the movies?" "Well yes, my love, and don't forget the popcorn and Raisinettes! You only become an adult once in your life and we will not let it be spoiled." So, we spent the day as planned and avoided the chaos around us until later that night. I had to admit I was glad to not think about it and spend hours laughing and eating junk food with her.

As a group, the Brainiacs got together to discuss our situation and what we need to do. What they decided on was, well, nothing. Our facility was built just for this very purpose. We had unlimited supplies of everything we needed. Our only real issue was the Tram System doors. We needed them open to get to the residential facility and to all of the other underground complexes around our zone. With them shut, we were literally shut off from everyone else. Those people trapped outside the doors have no access to our food, water, and medical supplies. The first order of business was setting up a crew whose sole purpose was to find a way to raise the doors back up where they belong. They rounded up the best engineers, some of which were the actual men who installed them in the first place, and then set them to the task. The next group they put together was issued the task of making contact with anyone. They were to try to use every resource they could come up with to contact either another facility or anyone up on the surface.

My main concern was my parents. They had to have been Top Side by the time the event occurred. My mom and dad are both scientists who study the effects of the changing climates on everything. They have been tracking the decline of certain insect and animal species, plants, and even the effects on humans. Four times a week, they take the Tram System to a hub that connects to the surface, well not actually the surface, it connects to a room under the Denver Airport with a door that lets them into the main terminal area. Travelers from Under Earth all have a microchip embedded in them that allows them access to an area that leads to the terminal entrance. From the substation, they can walk out on to the terminal platform and merge with other waiting commuters headed to towns for jobs.

Traveling is very dangerous in Top Side. There are still many groups or gangs that prey on anyone they choose. With no one to enforce laws, many people take what they want from whoever they want. Citizens with any kind of money or position have hired guards who go everywhere with them. My parents have a guard that escorts them to work four times a week. Many of the stores' warehouses and labs for Top Side are actually underground, just not nearly as far down as we are. The way our facility shook, way down here where we are, I can't imagine what they felt up there. My parents had to have made it to the lab by the time it happened. They left our living quarters at like six in the morning. The tram ride was at least twenty minutes, then they had to take a car and ride that for at least an hour into the main city. As long as they did not make any stops, take any detours off to a store or help a homeless person, they should have been in the lab. They should be okay. Right?

Late that evening, we all gathered at the cafe court area and chatted, commiserated, and generally began talking about our situation. I loudly cleared my throat, raised my hand like the teenage age girl I am trying to get the adults to listen to me, and asked, "Where are we going to sleep and, well, live, now that we can't get to our homes?" Everyone turned and looked to Dr. Pratte as if he was our leader. It was apparent he was, because we all looked to him for answers and that fact made him visibly uncomfortable.

"Um," he started. "I guess we should all try to figure something out short term. I am confident that it is only a matter of time until we get the doors open and can go back to our homes. From here on out, our lives will be all that we planned for after an event like this. There should be no more credits exchanged for goods or services. We have unlimited supplies that belong to us all. There is no need for currency anymore. This facility was built for us to live free and help each other. That phase begins now. As for housing, I suggest the mall. They have unused areas, and we can get mattresses and whatever we need from the warehouse." The crowd was muttering and nodding in agreement. The scientist and engineers opted to set up residency in their work areas. The nurses and doctors set up their living quarters on the third floor of the medical facility, which was only used for storage and had offices and conference rooms. Families chose an area, and everyone pitched in to get all the needed supplies.

Z and I raided the linen store and brought everyone sheets, blankets, towels, washcloths, and toiletry items. The two of us, being the youngest females there, decided to stay together. Of course, we chose the retro store in the mall. We made a pile of pillows and beans bag chairs to create an incredibly comfy bed for us. Z found a file cabinet from the back supply room to use as our dresser. She also went to the clothing shops and grabbed us several pairs of pajamas, bras, undies, and perfectly matched outfits, which she hung up on racks across the room. While she was out shopping in her true fashionista style, I set up our room and decorated it with twinkling lights hung from the ceiling, black lights, lava lamps, and glow in the dark stars above our bed. To me, it looked like a harem room mixed with a disco.

Z walked in, stopped abruptly, placed her hands on her hips, and asked, "Did the seventies throw up in here? Really, purple and gold? Come on give me a break!" "I worked really hard at this and no one ever appreciates what I do for them," I snapped at her without meaning to. She looked at me like I had lost my mind and cocked her right eye up at me like she always does when she feels I am acting childish. "I am sorry I snapped at you. It has been a stressful day, and I am so worried about my mom and dad," I explained.

She walked over to me and wrapped her arms around me. Her warmth and closeness made me feel so much better. I sighed and melted into her, wrapping my arm around her waist. We stood like that for a long time, taking comfort in each other. "The room is great, my love," she whispered. "I was just fucking with you." We spent that first night bouncing on our bean bag bed, pillow fighting, and eating junk food until we crashed and cuddled together under the glow of the black lights and lava lamps, with chiffon scarves blowing in the breeze from the air circulator.

Chapter Three: Settling In

Our lives were back to our normal routine in just a few days. Yes, we were all displaced from our living quarters, but everyone settled in nicely and made little homes for themselves and families. The groundskeepers kept up lush greenery around the facilities, the maintenance workers did their jobs, and so on. Wherever there was a person missing, we all took up the slack and the facility was running normally and on schedule. Everyone who lives here is here for a purpose, well except Zaynep and I. Even the two of us settled in to a routine. We had shifts at the cafe, we stocked the stores, and we even helped out on the farm with the cattle. We watched movies on Friday nights. We went to the dance on Saturdays and participated in the Sunday picnics after church.

Almost every night after our shift at the café, we would go work out in the gym and swim in the pool before heading home for the night. Z jogged every morning around the city center to the mall then out to the farm and back. All in all, it was about four miles. Not me, I like to sleep in. Before all this, I used to sleep until nine, eat some breakfast, and then get online for a while. School started at noon so there was no rush. I was the only student anyway, so Miss Scarlett was flexible with my hours. Z was already in college, which she did on exclusively on line. Days blurred into weeks and weeks into months with the doors still down and no contact with Top Side.

It was our turn to work the cafe. Six and a half months had passed since the Day the Earth Shook. We were all pitching in. The doctors, professors, and scientists just kept doing their thing. People who worked the greenhouse continued their jobs, and those that raised the livestock took care of them as usual. And still, we just filled in wherever we were needed and kept busy as much as we could all day. It kept our minds off of our parents. We began coordinating group dances and dinners, generally being social directors for the collective group. We continued to worked out every day in the gym at Z's insistence. She had always been a fitness fanatic. She looked the part too, tall, lean and muscular. I had a lot more curves. I was not obese; I preferred to call it fluffy. Z always tells me that I am just curvy and not chunky, but I am skeptical.

When I look at her perfect physique, I get self-conscious. She is always strutting around half-naked or even naked. She is very free and open, proud of her body, and sexually inquisitive. Me, well I have never even seen a boy my own age, much less talked to or touched one. Z called to me from the cafe kitchen. "Hey, everyone's gone, I am done in here." I responded, "Yep, just locked the door. You ready to go? Do we really have to go to the gym.? I am tired; my feet hurt and I'd rather go home." She came out of the kitchen and gave me that look that I know so well. "I have some frustrations to get out. I have not seen Eban in almost seven months. You just don't get it." She sighed as she grabbed her bag and walked out the door with me.

We arrived at the gym and it was deserted; we had it all to ourselves. Z promised me that if I would just run the treadmill with her for five miles, we could go home and I could pick the movie. Side by side we ran, both of us had our headphones on listening to music and we were sweating like we were in a sauna. The beeping of the timer saved me. We were done, thank God. We went to the changing room, stripped off our sweaty clothes and headed to the showers. I started the two shower heads and turned on the hot water as she dug through our bags for our wash clothes, body wash, shampoo, and conditioner. The entire room was full of steam when we entered the shower stall. Z placed her hands on the tile wall and stuck her head under the hot water, letting it flow over her. As I stepped in, she said, "Ah, please grab that loofa and scrub my back. Use the coconut wash. I love the smell of that one." I grabbed what she asked and squirted the coconut wash on my hands before rubbing it all over her back. The loofa made a squishy noise as I let it fill with hot water. I began to wash her back, shoulders, and butt. "I really miss Eban," she sighed as I washed her.

"Why? You very rarely see him anyway. I am sure it won't be too much longer until those assholes figure out how to get the doors open and you can go see him or whenever you want." She abruptly turned toward me and stated, "I'll show you why I miss him. Turn and put your hands up on the wall." "Really?" I asked. She grabbed me by my arms and turned me around. "Put them right here. And don't move. No matter what. You hear me?" She had taken my breath away. I just breathed out, "Yes." The hot water from the shower was running down my body, washing away the sweat from the work out and soothing my aches.

Z took the coconut body wash and began lathering up my back. She started at my neck, gently massaging her way down to my shoulders. She was close enough that I could feel her entire body pressing against mine. Her breath was hot on my neck as she whispered, "Do you want me to stop?" I had started to breathe so rapidly I could barely get out, "No." The steam surrounded us as the hot water cascaded down my body. My nipples were touching the tile and became very taut and ached in a way I have never experienced before. I could feel her nipples against my back, and they seemed to mimic mine.

She slowly slid her hand down the sides of my body, moving the sweet-smelling lather along my side over my hip bones then back up brushing the sides of my breasts. The sensation forced me to arch my back and lean into her, wanting more. She pressed herself into me and sucked my ear lobe in to her mouth. A gasp escaped my lips as I involuntarily pressed against her, my breasts heaving with the deep breaths I was taking and my heart beating out of my chest. Z began kissing and sucking my neck, moving down to my shoulder blades. She reached around and began washing my breasts, paying special attention to my nipples as she continued to kiss my neck, shoulders, and back. There were so many crazy feelings running through me that I had never experienced before. I didn't know what to do, but my body responded, it betrayed me as I wiggled and writhed against her touch, throwing my head back begging for more. She leaned back in to my ear and said, "This is why I miss Eban. This is how he makes me feel, the things we do. You get it now?" Z stepped away from me as I turned around, and she threw her head back in to the stream of hot water and began to wash her hair as if nothing had happened.

I was panting, wanting things I could not describe or understand. I just watched her wash herself. Seeing her in a completely different way than twenty minutes ago. Now the water running across her tight nipples made me ache deep inside, and I wanted to lick the drops off and suck those nipples between my lips. I wanted her to kiss me. I wanted to kiss her. I wanted to run my hands over her body like she had mine. What was wrong with me? I had to get control over myself. This was my best friend for my whole life! I suddenly realized that she was talking and I had not heard a thing except the sound of my heart beat and desire drumming in my ears. "Hello, are you even listening to me?" she said. I literally shook my head to clear it, and then I asked her to repeat what she had said.

Z looked at me, raised an eyebrow and said, "Oh, you did like it. Good. I was afraid I had gone too far and scared you or pissed you off. But, that is what sex stuff is like. I liked it too, which is why I had to stop so abruptly. I was scared I would go way too far." "I wasn't scared, it just surprised me, and I surprised myself with how I reacted. That was incredible! I get why you miss him now. I would miss that." I already did, as I was still watching her run her own hands over her body, surrounded by steam and covered in bubbles. Stop it, stop it, stop it, I told myself. I rinsed off, exited the shower, dried off, and quickly got dressed. What was I doing? Wanting to make out with her. What was wrong with me? I could still feel a throbbing ache in my groin and I felt so confused. There were no pillow fights that night. I professed to be exhausted and went to bed early. I dreamed all night of gentle lips covering every inch of my body while the sweet smell of coconut filled the air. My insides burned with aching need and desire.

We woke up the next morning wrapped up in each other as we always do, but for me it was awkward. "You must have been having some dream last night. I almost woke you but you looked so happy I just let you sleep," Z said first thing. "Yes, strange dream," I mumbled, fidgeting with my tank top. She ran her hand down the side of my face then cupped it in both her hands as she whispered, "I did not mean to upset you last night or make things weird between us. I love you, you are my best friend. I will never touch you like that again if it bothered you so much." I placed my hands on top of hers and raised my eyes to meet hers. I did not know what to say, but after being inseparable for eleven years, I decided to go with the truth.

"I really liked what we did last night. Maybe too much. I dreamt about it and much more last night. I was afraid to tell you that I was aroused by what you did." Z began to giggle, then lowered her face toward mine and gently kissed me on the lips. I kissed her back as her hands slid from my face to around the back of my neck. Her tongue gently pressed against my lips until I opened my mouth and let her in. Her tongue was warm, wet, and welcome. We lay there in bed just kissing and running our hands over each other.

Again, my body betrayed me and I began to wiggle and press myself against her, my nipples were so hard they ached for her attention. I just wanted her to suck on them and nibble and tug, but I dare not ask. This was her territory, not mine. I slowly brought my hand up to her small perky breast and brushed over it, grazing the nipple on the top of her night shirt. She made a small sound in the back of her throat and sucked my tongue deeper into her mouth. I was writhing and wiggling like I was covered in ants, yet she was controlled and deliberate with her touches. Z cupped my breast and grasped my nipple between her thumb and finger and gently tugged on it. This action caused a deep moan to escape from me and my back to arch pushing me into her. She pulled away, and then she placed ever so soft kisses on my lips, cheeks, eyes, forehead, and neck.

"Enough for today, okay? We need to slow this down. We are best friends and adding lovers to that will change everything. We could all be stuck down here for the rest of our lives or things could go back to normal tomorrow. I don't want to take your virginity. Playing around is okay, but until you know for sure what you want, I don't want to be the one to break your heart. " I was disappointed, frustrated and relieved all at the same time.

It had never occurred to me that she and I would or could be sexual with each other. All my sexual fantasies have always been about men I found attractive, actors on T.V. and Mr. Thorn, the head of security, is to die for. Both Z and I drool over him. He was tall, muscular, and blond with the most amazing blue eyes. Every area in the gym was coed. The sauna, the steam room, and even the showers, all of it. Ugh! We have spent many nights talking about the few times we have been working out at the gym at the same time as him. It never occurred to me that I could get so hot, wet, and bothered over a girl, especially my best friend. Z crawled out of our bean bag bed and headed to the bathroom. I always knew she was flawless and before it made me feel self-conscious, but now watching her walk away in her thong and half shirt made me tingle inside, in a way that was so very sweet.

We both got ready and dressed for the day without further discussion on our newfound intimacy. She acted perfectly normal, fluttering around like the social butterfly she is, chatting away about our plans for the rest of the day. We had duties at the agricultural center today. Dr. Pratte had made a schedule for all of us without real jobs, and we went from area to area learning how to take care of the livestock, run the greenhouse, help out in the clinic, restock the stores, and run the cafe. We liked the cafe, the greenhouse, and taking care of the animals the best. The only thing we did not like was Shane Tomlinson. He worked full-time with the livestock. He had not changed much from the dark, bad boy teen he had been before; in fact, he was almost as hot as Mr. Thorn but there was something creepy about him. His hair was long and hung over his face when it escaped his ponytail. His dark eyes were always staring, and he never seemed to blink.

He dated a few different women than I know of, but for the most part, he seemed antisocial. He never attended movie night or Sunday picnics. When I tried to invite him, he just smiled at me and said, "Enola, are you asking me out for a date? If you want to get me alone, all you have to do is ask." I guess the terrified look on my face amused him because he began to laugh. He caressed my face with one hand while sliding his other around the back of my neck. He leaned in and whispered in my ear, "One day I'll have you begging me to fuck you," then he walked away as if nothing had happened.

I never told Z about it and I convinced myself that he was just joking or trying to scare me, which he had accomplished. He did not usually talk much to us, but we caught him staring at us all the time with a lecherous grin that scared me even more after that encounter. He did not bother Z. She said that she would try him out one day, maybe, if he stopped being so creepy. She said she would probably let him kiss her a few times first but there was something about the way he looked at us that really kind of scared her yet intrigued her too. Six months later, he showed his true deep dark side.

A year into our confinement...

"Come on sweetie, move it." Z begged me. I was cuddling a new born calf after bottle-feeding him. He was all black soft and smelled of hay. I just loved the baby animals. ""Okay, I am coming. I just need to grab on more bale of hay for momma here, and I will meet you at the gate. Okay?" She stomped off in the direction of the facility exit gate while I climbed up into the loft and started unwrapping a bale of hay. The bales are shrink wrapped and placed in the storage loft that is climate controlled to make them last longer. It took me at least fifteen minutes when I finally had the hay unwrapped and placed the hook in it to drag it down to the stall for the new momma cow to enjoy.

As I backed out of the stall while brushing hay off of my jeans, suddenly there was a large muscular arm around my neck and a hand hooked through my belt dragging me backward. I was so taken by surprise that I did not even scream, I just grabbed ahold of the board on the wall and started trying to kick whoever was behind me. I did not use a lot force at first because my first thought was that it was some kind of joke. Shane pulled me tight to his chest and growled in my ear, "I see how you two look at me. I look at you like that, too." His breath was hot on my neck and smelled like smoke and alcohol. He was very strong and held me tight to his body. He smelled of sweat and hay.

Shane began to kiss my neck and moved his hand down to my breast and roughly began to squeeze it. I could feel his erection against my back, solid and wanting. With one hand, he ripped my shirt open and tore my bra in half, exposing my breasts. His voice was deep and rugged as he groaned and whispered, "Oh, look at those babies." His breathing was getting more rapid as he slid his other had around to the front of my jeans and began fumbling with my belt.

That is when I began to kick at his legs with some real force. I wiggled and struggled against him trying to break free from his grip. "Please Shane, stop it. I don't want this, please stop, you're hurting me." Tears began to run down my face and my pleas came out like sobs. "Keep squirming honey," he panted, "That is only making this hotter for me." He managed to get my belt undone and my pants unzipped while I twisted in his grip. He slid his hand down my underwear and briefly stroked me. He was grinding himself against me as he said, "It is true, no hair anywhere but your head. That will make licking your pussy so much nicer." He grabbed a horse lead from the wall, pulled my arms behind my back and tied my hands together while I cried and begged him to stop. "I won't tell anyone Shane, you were drinking, and you are freaked out like all of us about our predicament and lonely. I get it, it is not too late to just stop and let me go."

Shane chuckled a bit then kissed me hard, forcing his tongue in my mouth while grinding his penis against me. "You want this as much as I do, you little slut. You watch me and tease me every time you see me. Who else is even close to your age that deserves some tight ass virgin pussy? It will be our secret, trust me, you will like it and come back for more and more. I am willing to oblige and teach you how to satisfy a man like a woman should. Get on your knees and lick those lips, baby, I want them wet."

He bent down and roughly tool my nipple into his mouth and made a groan as he looked at me and pressed me down on the floor on my knees. He pulled a knife from his belt and cut my shirt and bra the rest of the way off. My cheeks were red with embarrassment, fear, and anger. Shane began to undo his belt and unzipped his zipper. He was not wearing anything beneath and his erect penis was free, only inches from my face. I was struggling and twisting all around trying to get away from him while he slapped my face with his erection. He laughed a bit and then became impatient and slapped me hard with his hand. "Enough playing bitch, suck it. Make me cum and then I will show you how good Shane can make you feel."

He pinched my face with one hand while trying to force his dick in my mouth, just as the lights went out. "Fuck, what happened to the lights?" he growled. I was furiously trying to work my hands free. He was still holding me down on my knees with one hand while trying to maneuver his erection back into his pants. He was so close all I could smell was sweat, animals, and musk. I thought I was going to throw up or pee myself. I was so scared I did the first thing that came to mind and head butted him directly in the groin. He let me and his penis go and stumbled back a few steps. That is when I heard a loud cracking noise and the sound of his body crumbling to the floor. Z appeared at my side. She looked as scared as me, but there was also a look in her eyes that I had never seen. "You okay Honey? You have to get up. We need to get rid of him."

Z untied my hands, and I tied my shirt around my breast to cover myself up. "Get rid of him? Let's just get out of here," I said. "Then what? Just go on business as usual? He will do it again, if not to us, to some other poor woman. No one will believe us. He is well-liked and handsome. They will say you wanted it and changed your mind. He is already really hurt and bleeding from the gash on his head. I can see his brains, Enola. I hit him with an ax. It was the only thing I could find. We will throw him down the old drilling hole and no one is the wiser. Do you trust me Enola? You know when I said I would give him a try, well I tried just letting him kiss me and see how that went. He has been rubbing up against me and dusting my breasts for weeks. He tried to fuck me last week, and it got really rough when I told him that kissing was enough, and I refused to suck his dick. He threw me on the ground and started to rip my clothes off, just like you. Thank God someone came around looking for him and started to call him from the gate. This won't stop," she assured me. I couldn't believe all that happened to her and she had not told me about it before this. I nodded and followed her lead.

We could not move him ourselves, so we tied his arms and used a horse to drag him to the back field that has an old drilling hole. There are several all over the fortress. Holes were drilled to the Earth's core. Some had not gone all the way and were abandoned. We rolled him in and raked over the drag marks, cleaned up the blood, and went home. She held me all night as I cried. See why I was not ready to tell you about the one and only murder that has occurred in our perfect little paradise? We were the ones who did it. It was surprising easy to deny knowing where he went, and after a while, everyone stopped looking and asking. A lot of rumors came out about angry, jealous husbands and his drinking, aggressiveness, strange behavior, and drug issues, and then, after a while, he was forgotten, except by me.

Chapter Four: Life Goes On

Our tutor before the event was Miss Scarlett. Yes, we giggle every time we say her name. Clue is one of my favorite video games and Z plays it with me all the time. Plus, you know the whole Gone with the Wind thing. I wish she had a husband or boyfriend named Rhett but her boy toy is named BOB, you know, Battery Operated Boyfriend. We have never even seen her talk to a man; she is always too serious and shy. She does have a cat who we begged her to name Rhett, and she finally acquiesced. Now that we can no longer go to school online since the computer system has no archives to hook up to, she has become our full-time teacher. Since it is only me in the last year of school before college and Z who wanted to study psychology as her college major, Miss Scarlett had an easy time with the transition.

There have never been any other children here but us- me from birth and Z since she was ten. The closest people to our age are ten years older than me, like Shane was. I think about him at least once a day. I know it is not healthy for me. I just can't seem to forget it. I really can't explain how I feel either. I don't feel guilty, he was trying to rape me for goodness sakes. He tried to do the same to Z also. There was proof he drank too much alcohol and smuggled drugs in from Top Side. When people realized he was missing, they searched the entire facility and then the room he was living in near the barn. In his room, they found popular recreational drugs from Top Side. There were a lot of them. He also had a lot of pornography and items that some of the women in town were missing. You know, underwear, bras, jewelry. It started a lot of tension in some married couples' lives. Accusations were thrown all over about affairs and rapes. I have to stop thinking about it. What I did to him and what he almost did to me. Was an attempted rapist deserving of death?

We went to the library three times a week and studied. Of course, our library is all computerized, but that information is all in the hard drive so we did not need the World Internet to access it. So, Z was studying Psychology, like she was not already a professional at manipulating people, but she wanted more power.. I wanted to be a Veterinarian and work in the Agricultural Center with all of our livestock. There are so many issues with raising animals underground and with raising people. We had ultraviolet lights and sun lamps in the greenhouse and the animal pens. We have the same type of solar system for our human population, too. The problem is that they are in the housing facilities that we can no longer get to.

Dr. Pratte advised everyone to utilize the Agricultural Center's sun lamps at least once every few weeks to keep up with the nutrients they provided. It was a few people coming to do so that saved Z the day that Shane had her pinned to the ground and was ripping her clothes off. It was three nurses and a doctor from the medical unit. We always made their food extra special when they came to the cafe on the days we worked there.

Nurse Lori always commented on how they get such great service when we are on shift, and Doctor Jack raves about the beautiful presentation of my salads. We can't help it, we almost hover over them. They are life savers by profession, and they saved a young girl from being raped and maybe beaten or killed without even knowing they did it. Nurse Lori had been seen with Shane a lot at the park and the cafe. I don't know if she misses him or not. I wonder if she knows how dangerous he was and if they were involved. She does not have Z's look at all. Lori is the hometown girl next door with freckles and a few extra pounds. She always has a smile on her face and a cute giggle. What did she have in common with Shane? I have to stop thinking about him.

Three years in New Eden…

Z loves the days we work at the cafe. She is a natural at fluttering from table to table like a butterfly engaging in conversations with everyone. Everyone loves her, and she loves the attention that waiting tables provides her. When we get home, she fills me in on what everyone tells her, which is amazingly a lot. I told you she has a way with people, and they seem to tell her anything she wants to know. By the end of our shift, she knows who is sleeping with who, which engineers are starting to lag behind in their duties, what illnesses and injuries have happened to who, and what progress, if any, has been made on the communication with Top Side issues and getting the doors open.

"Come on, come on, come on, we need to get to the gym," she urges. "If we don't hurry, Mr. Thorn will be done working out, and I, for one, do not want to miss seeing him shower." Yes, I have to admit that the two of us have been purposely working out at the same time as him and finishing at the same time also in order to hit the showers at the same time.

It took Z two years to get me to get in the shower naked, while he was also in there naked. I finally conceded, and I have to admit that watching him, as discreetly as we possibly could, was amazing. I had never seen an actual live man naked before, and he was such an appealing specimen. He had to be suspicious by now, after a year that we have been doing it on purpose, but I think he liked it, too. After all, he had a full view of us showering, too, and come on, what guy would not be flattered that we wanted to watch him while he got to watch us? We touched each other while he was in there, but nothing too hot and heavy. Not that Z didn't try to talk me into doing a lot more in front of him, because she tried all the time.

I know she was hoping that if we started getting sexual with each other while he could see us, maybe he would join in. I did not think he would, with him being in his early thirties and a respected authority figure with a wife, but he never covered himself up or acted like he did not want us in there. He never altered his workout schedule and said nothing to us about it. Sometimes, he would turn away from us and turn on the cold water, acting as if he was rinsing off. Z said that meant we got him excited and he was trying to hide that fact from us. See, a nice, respectable man, and oh so hot.

Z and I often discussed why no other children have been born here, especially in the three years we have been cut off. Mr. Thorne has been married to his wife for six years, and there it is predominately couples living here. Granted, two-thirds of our population is over forty-five, and their kids were grown and out on their own before they moved to New Eden. But there were at least thirty-five women of childbearing age here at the beginning. After all of the deaths, I believe we are down to fifteen, not counting Z and I. So why have none of the women gotten pregnant? I decided to ask Dr. Pratte about it.

Dr. Pratte sat at his usual table in the cafe surrounded by the usual suspects. By that, I mean that his lab crew always eats together. I thought this was a perfect time to raise my question about the lack of pregnancy. As I delivered the blueberry lemon tart to the table, I cleared my throat and began. "Um. Excuse me, Dr. Pratte, may I ask you a question about something that has really been bothering me?" He looked over the top of his glass at the doctors sitting around him and then up at me. "Why of course Enola. What is on your mind?" I pulled out an empty chair and sat down at their table. I leaned in a little and lowered my voice so that none of the other customers could overhear me. "Well, I find it very strange that I am the only child ever born here, especially now that we are stuck here. Have the women become sterile, or is it forbidden or something?" They all began to chuckle over my question.

Dr. Pratte took off his glasses and took me by the hand. He looked around the table and received nods from the other doctors. He took a breath and seemed to think about what he was about to say. "Enola, we have had many discussions and meetings about our population. As you know, the people brought down here were all special in their own way and had skills to help keep our community thriving. Everyone has a purpose. We wanted to keep all people represented and keep history alive. Everyone but you was been born and raised Top Side. We were all exposed to radiation, amoebas, and diseases. Only you are pure. Now that we have extinguished all efforts to be able to go back to Top Side, we are looking at expanding our population. We have to be very careful who we breed. We do not want anyone inferior here. Do you understand what I mean?"

I was dumbfounded and hoped that I did not understand. Is he saying what I think? Do they like the idea of all that genetic manipulation stuff to have perfect humans? I was unsure what to say, then I asked some questions. "First off, you said everyone here has a purpose to be here. What about Z and I? Is her purpose to decorate and mine to study?" Again, the looks around the table, and they are all nodding toward Dr. Pratte like they are encouraging him.

"Enola. Z was predetermined for psychology and international studies from birth. She was chosen to be stationed here as your companion. None of this was necessary for you to know. If you two had not become fast friends, they would have sent another. You were born here. There are one or two pure born in every Fortress. Pure borns have the purpose of studying how the effects of life underground affect you and your ability to populate our new life with more like you."

I felt my heart and jaw drop. "Does Z know? Is she just pretending to be my friend? What am I, breeding stock?" Dr. Byrde, sitting to my right, clasped my hand and turned me toward her. She smiled and said, "Come on dear, calm down. Z was only told about how special you are when she turned eighteen. She loves you as we all do. It was planned that when you were of age there would be a couple of boys like you who were sent from other facilities for you to choose from. You are the first pure born. That is why you were named Evangeline, Eve. That is why our fortress is called New Eden. The majority of the elders decided that to call you Eve was blasphemous. The same thing would occur in all the other fortresses when their females turned of age. You would all have your choice, the pick of the litter. Then we could study what your offspring would be. But it would be your choice and your baby. We would require nothing else from you, and protect you and your children at all costs. You are our future. The walls fell before it was your time. The plans for the study and the experiment were lost."

I pulled my hand away from her and stood up so quickly my chair hit the table behind me. They were all staring at me and waiting. I did not know what to do. I just ran. I ran out of the cafe down through the town center.

I passed the hospital and the lab, and I made a beeline for the barns. I threw myself into a pile of hay and sobbed. For the rest of the tale, the other horrible truths never occurred to me. Now I knew why I felt like everyone treated me differently. Why I looked different and why I was the only kid here. I decided after hours lying there that I would not ever talk to them about it again. Their plan had failed; I would not be their breeding stock so they had no use for me and I was fine with that.

Around midnight, Zeynep found me. She looked like she had been crying, too. She ran to the hay pile, jumped in, and held me tight. "I was so worried about you! I have been looking everywhere. You scared me to death. Don't ever run off on me again." We both started crying and just held each other until we calmed down. I stood up and brushed the hay from my faded jeans and halter top. "I just want to go home, okay?" I told her and Z stood, performed the same hay removal ritual, took my hands, kissed me long and hard, then started walking home. We did not say another word to each other the whole way back. We just held hands and made our way home.

Two months later, Z decided to breach the subject. "So, are you ever going to tell me what the old assholes told you that made you run off and scare me shitless?" Really, this is how she was going to play it? I took a deep breath, rolled my eyes, and tried to figure out what to say to my best friend slash girlfriend slash guardian. "They explained to me my purpose here in New Eden. And also your purpose to be my friend and protect me. Oh, yeah, I forgot, I am also the sacred cow who was supposed to be the finest breeding stock. Until "The Day the Earth Shook." Now I am useless. Does that cover it?"

She placed her hands on each side of my face and pulled me into a soft lingering kiss. "You could never be useless my dear. I never knew any secrets about you until I had been your best friend for eight years. Yes, it all came as a shock to me that I was only placed here because genetically we are deemed compatible, and they figured they would need someone with my genetically engineered skills here. Not just for you, but for everyone. Please tell me we are still us!" She started to kiss me again and grind her body into mine. I could not help myself. I melted and kissed her more fervently and began to run my hands all over her body.

My pulse was racing, my nipples so hard they hurt, and my panties were getting rather moist. I wanted more, more, more. I grasped the bottom of her barely-there half shirt and pulled it over her head. Of course, as always, she was not wearing a bra. My breasts were too large to go without. I ran my hands over her succulent nipples and began kissing and sucking my way down to them. She arched her head back as I took a nipple in my mouth. "Oh, yes," she whispered. "Don't stop Enola, lower". I looked up at her and she smiled and nodded. We have never done more than nipple play as she calls it. She has once in a while rubbed her own clit while I ravished her breasts. But that is it. She always stopped it there. Now I know why.

I was destined to be a bitch and produce pure borns for them, not indulge in sex play with a girl. Well, indulge is what I was planning to do. As I kissed my way past her breasts, I unbuttoned her shorts and began sliding them over her slim hips and let them drop to the floor. Next, I slid my hand down the front of her panties and immediately discovered a very wet slit. I had no idea what to do, but I began to rub and probe and the more she wiggled and moaned, the hotter I got and the more aggressive I became with my fingers. My kisses were getting lower as I began to kneel in front of her. I could smell a delicious mustiness and began to moan myself. I had one finger moving inside of her and my thumb caressing her clit.

She was shaved bare and so very soft on my face. Z placed her hands on my shoulders and pushed me further down. I was anxious to get there also. I had dreams about this over and over, but she had never let things get this far before. I moved my thumb out of the way and inserted a second finger inside her. Oh, she was so wet and warm and grinding against me. I was just as wet and just following her lead. I licked her slit and rubbed my thumb around her clit again. She arched and moaned and ground against me even more. The smells and the taste made me even hotter. I began to suck, lick, tickle, and massage with my tongue and thumb while thrusting my finger inside her. Her juices were all over my lips, chin, and hand. It was ecstasy.

She grabbed the back of my head and thrust into her harder while grinding against me until suddenly she cried out and just held me there tight. I was shaking with desire and want. She grabbed my shoulders and pulled me into a standing position. She was panting and flushed and I knew I was the same. "I am sorry Enola. I should never have allowed that to happen. It is forbidden for anyone to have sex with you. They would send me away if they knew all that we did before this. I cannot return the favor, but I can talk you through doing it yourself." All during her speech, she was caressing my breasts and kissing me. Her speech ruined the mood. Though the taste and smell of her still lingered on my lips, I declined to play with myself and just enjoyed kissing for a while longer. Knowing that my sex life or lack thereof is a topic of community discussion had cooled down my desire.

BOOM BOOM BOOM

It is getting much louder now, and the theory is that it means whatever it is, it is getting very close. The sound started reaching us over a year ago. There is no telling how long they have been digging. As that ominous sound gets louder and begins to make our world vibrate with its power, we all huddle in the main square. I don't know why we all ended up gathering together in the same location, but we did. How stupid that is. It reminded me of old horror movies where the victims made it easy for the psycho killer or vampire or zombie to get everyone all at once. For the life of me, I could not verbalize my fears, even to Z. We shared all of our secrets, our fears, and our dreams but this I could not find a way to express without sounding like a scared child after a nightmare.

I suddenly felt alone, lonely and as if I had no one, no faith, no dreams, and no future. A very foreign place for the likes of me. Boom, boom, boom. I grasped Blaze by her hand. I desperately needed to feel some kind of comfort, but this feeling of doom had overcome me. Even the familiarity and warmth of her touch did not penetrate this darkness. I think that I had never actually been depressed in my entire life. I had been scared, confused, and awkward but never depressed. This feeling was like a premonition instead of what was happening at this very moment. That is the only way I can attempt to explain it. I wish I had only known how correct my premonition was and said something, but I did not. You cannot change the past, but the future is open to all interpretations. I could have saved some lives and some sanity, but I was a coward. Oh, well. There is no going back.

Chapter Five: Something Wicked This Way Comes

"**Enola! Enola? Let go of my hand,** you are hurting me. Honey, look at me. You are as pale as a ghost. Don't buy into all this mass hysteria. You know these people panic over the slightest little thing. There could have been some type of natural disaster. An earthquake. A volcano. Something. We may have been the only fortress affected. That sound is the sound of our saviors coming to rescue us." The look on Z's face told me everything I needed to know. She did not even believe the shit she was shoveling.

"If it was just us, and it is our people coming to get us. then why would they be coming from Top Side? You know that would be exposing our way of life and all of us around the world would be affected. Our people would find a way through the tunnels, not from Top Side. This is something else, and we all know it. If my father was up there, it would not have taken him seven years to come for me." Mrs. Bryant whipped her head around and stared into my eyes with hatred and intensity. "What did you just say? What? Tell me!" She is just scared, defended Z. "No, she is right!" Mrs. Bryant shouted in the middle of the town square. "Out of the mouth of babes! The good and holy people who know we are down here would never risk everything and everyone to tunnel from above!" she shouted to the now listening crowd.

Mrs. Bryant stepped up upon the center stage, arms raised to the sky, and engaged the people with a face of determination and despair. "The tunnels. Our tunnels are the way in and out throughout our fortresses. A stranger from above is not here to save us but to take our souls. All is lost, my friends. The rapture is upon us or was, and we were left behind. Our indiscretions, our sins, and our impure ways have set themselves upon us like a wolf to an unguarded lamb. We set ourselves apart from the rest of the world as if we were better, special. We have no one to blame but ourselves. Our pride and self-importance have been our downfall. Repent and beg the Lord to save your souls before we are devoured by the evil one." Her body began to shake, her eyes rolled in her head, and she fell to the floor. What a fucking drama queen. Those wrapped up in her frenzy ran to her side while those who were sick of her shit returned to the conversations they were having before her righteous rant.

Dr. Pratte appeared out of the crowd and made his way slowly and with determination onto the stage. For the last seven years, he has been our rock. He was always working on ways to find communication with others, keeping all of our systems in working order, and calming us in times of panic. This is one of those times. The past seven years have taken a toll on him. I always thought of him as old, but now he appeared to be ancient. His skin was thin and translucent. He was hunched over and frail. Not the man he used to be.

He cleared his throat and raised his eyes to meet those in the crowd. Running his hand through his gray gossamer hair, he sighed. It was clear to everyone in attendance that he was not looking forward to speaking to us today. There would be no coddling and no reassurance that we are fine coming from his wrinkled lips on this day.

"As I look out over you all today, while you huddle together, scared and confused, I find myself at a loss for words. My staff has spent countless hours over the past years trying to figure out where we stand in the order of things. What occurred at Top Side? We still have no clue. How can we do anything but speculate? Unlike Mrs. Bryant, we are not convinced that it was an act of God. Could we be the only fortress affected? Yes. Would our fellow scientists try to reach us through Top Side? Well, only if the rail system and tunnels were completely destroyed or contaminated with some type of radioactive waste. We have no clue what or who is coming. By the sounds and vibrations, we can only discern that there are heavy equipment and explosives involved. Why do they only dig at night? Again, we can only speculate at this point." Dr. Pratte began to pace slowly across the stage and bowed his head again.

He took a long sip from his water bottle, wiped his liver-spotted hand across his brow, and continued. "I can tell you what we do know. They are intelligent and educated enough to know where we are and to operate the equipment necessary to accomplish their task to get down to us. At the rate they are progressing, they will reach our inner perimeter in a week to ten days. Are they human or mutations? Alien or gods? Friend or foe? What are their intentions once they arrive? These are the questions that plague us now. My friends, please listen to me now. We must be prepared for anything. My team and I will attempt to pinpoint the area that they will breach. At that time, we can evacuate that section. Our thoughts are that to delay the inevitable long enough to discern their origin and intentions before they find us."

He went on, "Once we narrow down the area they will come through, we can all work together to make that section look deserted and uninhabited. While they look around and descend upon us, we can observe them on the monitoring system within the compound. This way, we could get some kind of idea of what we need to do and what they want from us. I will call a meeting as soon as we have available information. My team and or our security team will make initial contact when and if it is necessary. Please, my friends, stay calm and work together." He walked off of the stage with less purpose than when he climbed it. His head bent, his back hunched, and there was a slight tremor in his hands. The gathering was silent as he walked through the crowd and back toward his lab. It was much less dramatic than Mrs. Bryant's performance but ultimately more terrifying. Blaze and I did not stick around to wallow in the muck.

"Let's go to the gym. I bet Mr. Thorn is there. He was not at the meeting," she said. "Really! That is what you are thinking about now? I am scared, Z," I admitted. All she did was cock her head and give me the mischievous smile and I knew I was done for. "It is just the thing to help release tension and stress." We giggled the whole way there, almost skipping arm and arm. So okay, watching that fine specimen of a man shower would take my mind off of our latest woes.

We skipped past the workout part altogether and went straight to the showers. There was no giggling any longer. Both of us were undressed before we even made it to the locker room. My mind was on some fun play with her. We had never done more than some fondling and kissing until last week. I am about to explode. I watch her masturbate at night sometimes and wish she would finish me off. It makes me ache and long for release. Today was going to be the day, I could feel it.

As we entered the shower room, oh wow, there he was. It was like he was waiting for us. He was just standing there, water cascading over his shoulders. He was facing us and it was very easy to see that he was happy to see us. Z walked straight toward him without missing a beat or saying a word. She stopped only inches from him and took that tilted cocky stance of hers. Head cocked to the side, she bit her lower lip, looked down at his protruding thick erection, and said, "Is that for me, big boy?" He took a shuddering deep breath while his eyes took in every inch of her. Surprisingly, I was not jealous but extremely aroused to the point of almost panting. My nipples were so hard they hurt, and I reached up to caress them. He stared into her blues eyes and said, "Why do you girls do this to me all the time? Do you have any idea what it has taken me to ignore you for six years? I can't take it any longer. Make a move Zeynep." Then, he whispered. "Touch me and I'll give in. Please touch me."

Z glanced over her shoulder at me and instantly saw my need. I was still touching myself and biting my lower lip. I wanted one of them or both of them to take me to places I had yet explored. She looked back at him, wrapped her arms around his neck, and said, "As long as you understand that Enola is a virgin and is going to remain that way. She can touch us, you can touch her, but no penetration with her, mister." "Deal," was all I heard and they were tangled up, hands groping, tongues licking, and body parts entwined. She stretched out a hand in my direction and beckoned me with one finger. I felt as if I floated over toward them.

I pressed my naked body up against her back, reached my arms around her, and ran my fingers through his hair. He broke off from nuzzling her breasts, looked over her shoulder, and begged, "Touch me, Enola, please. You are so fucking hot. Both of you are. Kiss each other." I slid to their sides where Z wrapped her arms around my neck and pulled me into a long, deep, satisfying kiss. She moved down my neck to my nipples, licking, sucking, and nuzzling, all the while stroking his throbbing hard cock. His gaze never left mine. I could tell he wanted to do the same things to me. I ran my hand along his jawline and kissed his shoulder. He smelled of soap and lust, and my clit was hot and throbbing with a need that had never been realized.

Z stopped touching me, dropped to her knees, and took him into her mouth. I moved around behind his back and pressed myself against him. The warm water ran all over us, and steam filled the room. I began to kiss his back and shoulders while using my tongue to lick the water droplets from his skin. He grabbed my hand. He placed our intertwined hands in Z's hair and began rocking them back and forth with the rhythm she already created. I moved to his side while his other hand grabbed my hair and pulled my head back. I groan as he kissed me hard and slipped his tongue in my mouth. He moved his lips to my throat and sucked and nuzzled his way down to my nipples. We let go of Z's hair as she turned toward me and buried her head in my crotch. His mouth and tongue working wonders on my breasts while her tongue flicked my clit.

She began to suck on my lips and I gasped, arching into her. Mr. Thorn was panting now and seemed almost frantic in his caressing and sucking. She licked her way up my abdomen and met his lips on my left nipple. They began to kiss and grind their bodies together, which kind of then pushed me out of the way. Then it happened. They told me to leave. I could not believe my ears. My heart was beating so strong and hard I could barely understand the words coming out of her mouth. "You know why," is all she said to me. I was devastated. There I was, on the brink of finding out what the real pleasures of having sex could be, and she stole it away from me. Hot tears burned my eyes as I attempted to keep them in check. I knew there was no arguing, and if I did, I would just ruin everything for them too.

Mr. Thorn picked her up as she wrapped her long tan legs around his waist. He pushed her against the dripping shower wall while forcing her hands high above her head. "Leave!" she screamed at me. And I did. As I ran out the door, I could still hear her screams of pleasure and his panting grunts echoing in my head. I threw on my clothes while almost running. I could not get out of there fast enough. My need was no longer drumming in my brain and loins. I was embarrassed and hurt. I decided I need to do something of my own, something only I know about. So here we are. I am chronicling the events since "The Day the Earth Shook," for whoever one day finds it. Who knows, I may be wasting my time. When the diggers get here, we may discover that the world is just fine and that we spent the last almost seven years worrying for nothing. Then again, it could be strange creatures coming to eat our brains. Oh, wait, that would be zombies. After today, my writings will be what is currently happening, as long as I still have a brain. I crack myself up sometimes.

"Chapter Six: Discoveries"

Lying on her bed of bean bags and throw pillows, Enola gazed at the ceiling where they had pasted glow in the dark planets and stars. While Zeynep was out screwing a married man in the gym shower room, Enola decided to use glow in the dark paint to add some improvements to their view. She began to crawl her way out of our pile of fluff and head down to the craft store. Of course, it took a few minutes to make her way to the floor. They went a little overboard when assembling what they call their "Princess Tower."

The hardwood floor is cold on her bare feet as she tumbles out of the tower. She picked herself up off of the floor and searched around for where her sandals landed the last time she kicked them off. The right one was located almost immediately since it was under her knee when she hit the floor. The left shoe was nowhere in sight. Lighting in the room were LED Christmas lights and plastic tiki torches. These were not optimal for locating a missing black sandal but perfect for making out or dancing. She finally spied it under a pile of rose petals and scarfs.

Yes, they are pampered here in their little domain. The thought makes her giggle and pushes her earlier woes further away. Enola never has been able to stay upset or angry long. It seems pointless and counterproductive to hold on to negative feelings. How could she be upset crawling off of a pile of satin, silk, and cotton in a softly lit room that smells of jasmine and sage? And don't forget the flower petals scattered all over the floor and her favorite music playing! Impossible.

She slides on her newly found sandal and skips all the way out the door and down the walkway toward the craft store. She suddenly realized that something was wrong. It was silent out of her living quarters. No banging. No digging and no noise from City Center either. The intruders never stop their work at night. Not since the very first day when they started to hear them. All thoughts of painting lotus flowers left her head as she was sprinting back to the gym to warn them.

Z was already dressed and in the City Center when Enola located her. Mr. Thorn was nowhere in sight. It appeared that most of the residents of New Eden were gathered around the center stage marveling at the sudden lack of noise coming from Top Side. Dr. Pratte was standing along with everyone else, gazing at the ceiling. Father Joe was at his side so close their heads were almost touching. He looked as if he was whispering something to the doctor that he did not wish anyone else to hear. Enola stood next to Blaze and slid her hand into hers. Z squeezed her hand and whispered, "It all just suddenly stopped when I was on my way home. Creepy isn't it?" Enola nodded in agreement, hesitant to talk and disturb the hush that had fallen over the town.

Dr. Pratte climbed the stairs to center stage where he had stood a few hours earlier. He raised his eyes to the crowd and asked in a steady voice, "Has anyone seen Riley, sorry, Mr. Thorn? He did not answer his radio when I tried to call him a little while ago." Z tugged at Enola's hand and glared at her, warning her not to answer that question. Enola mouthed just one word to her. "Riley?" Then began to giggle until Zaynep jabbed her elbow into her ribs. The radio attached to Dr. Pratte's black belt suddenly came to life with the head security officer's voice, startling the entire assembly.

"Dr. Pratte. Dr. Pratte. This is Thorn. Come in Sir." "Riley, we need you to report to the City Center immediately. We have a complication. Contact all of your men and have them report also. Dr. Pratte out." Dr. Pratte raised his head and addressed the crowd, "Well, the first problem is solved. Let's hope everything else goes as quickly and easily." Everyone began talking at once. Some were asking questions directed at Dr. Pratte, others were talking amongst themselves. Z turned to Enola and said, "Let's go home, we can't be where they can find us. Riley will fill me in later about what goes on down here." Enola raised a brow, "So we are calling him Riley now?" "Well," Z whispered, "It sounds better than screaming Mr. Thorn when I was cumming." The girls walked back to their room, arm in arm, laughing, and tickling each other to where Enola laid out her plans for painting lotus flowers down the walls and a pond on the floor.

She has never had a lesson but can beautifully paint or draw anything she wants. She also has discovered throughout these years cut off from Top

Side and the Internet that she can play any musical instrument she picks up. Z explained to her that a lot of people are artsy like her. There just aren't any others in New Eden. Enola, not knowing any differently, believed her and loved to paint things for everyone in town. Painting, drawing, playing musical instruments, and taking apart broken items and making them work again were some of her passions. So far there has not been anything that Enola is not good at. Enola is the only one that does not notice it and find it strange and unusual. But then, everyone else except Z was here when Enola arrived in New Eden.

Zaynep insisted that the lotus flowers be purple just like Enola's eyes. She sat cross-legged on the floor and periodically handed Enola paint, brushes, and rags while they chatted about future plans for decorating. Enola decided to ask Blaze about some comments that were made to her as nonchalantly as she could. She was not sure how to ease them into the conversation, but she knew from experience that asking Z questions she did not want to answer would not turn out in her favor.

Enola worked up her courage and said, "You know what struck me as odd? Last week when I was painting that mural at the rectory for Father Joe, Mrs. Bryant stopped by and watched me for a few minutes. She seemed to be acting odd even for her. I kept checking my brush strokes because she was looking at my painting like there was something wrong. As she left she commented to Father Joe. She said, 'You would think that her talents would be more critical to our existence than aesthetics.' What could she have meant by that?" I asked Z. She just stared at me. I could see the wheels turning in her head while she tried to figure out what to say to me. I decided to just keep going.

"Was my DNA messed with like yours? Was I genetically programmed also? And if so, did it go wrong and I did not become what they intended?" Z looked as if she was going to faint, she was pale and began to pace around. "Please Enola. Don't push this. All I truly know is that you are the first pure born person since the garden of Eden. I never asked any more questions. By the time they filled me in on my genetic predetermination, I was overwhelmed. We were already like sisters and I did not want to know anymore. I knew the day would come when you would ask me questions and I did not want to be the one to tell you anything. I, of all people, know how you feel about genetic experiments and manipulations. I did not want you to judge me or us. It is of no consequence now. Their days of playing God are over. Just accept that you are special and let's go on. Okay?"

I realized that I could not get any further information out of her and I did not want to put anything between us. She was all I really had here or anywhere for that matter. I decided then and there that I would have to find out anything further from snooping in the lab. They had to keep records of everything they have done here. I could show interest in the lab and learning what goes on there. What the hell, I am the golden child, if they want me to show potential they should indulge my curiosity. Right? I figured I would speak to the scientists and charm my way in, starting tomorrow. Z was still staring at me waiting for an answer. "Well, I guess if all I am good for is aesthetics, I better get to work on finishing the mural. Mrs. Bryant can kiss my ass."

Z burst out one of her best smiles and began to laugh. We laughed together until I tossed some paint off of my brush in her direction. Yes, I did it on purpose. She immediately picked up a rag and chucked it at my head. It all went downhill from there. By the time we settled in a heap together on the floor, both of us were covered in paint and sweating. Good thing I always put a tarp down before I get started or we would have had an impossible mess to clean up. She placed her hands around my neck and pulled me close into a kiss. She whispered into the crook of my neck, "If I wasn't worried about getting paint into some possibly painful areas, I would absolutely force you to lick me from head to toe." The very thought of that quickened my breathing and heartbeat. I tilted her head up and continued the kiss.

She had paint all over her neck do I skipped that part and lifted her shirt over her head. The lacy red bra she had on was useless. It barely even covered her nipples. Seeing them made me give out a little groan of pleasure. It had a snap in front that released practically on its own with the slightest pressure from my tongue. As it sprung open, she arched herself forward to meet my mouth. Her skin was salty and sweet at the same time, and she smelled of paint and jasmine. As I savored her right nipple in my mouth, I ran my thumb over her left one. They instantly became hard and poked out further. She was letting out small gasps and groans as I sucked harder and began twisting her nipple between my thumb and forefinger.

Suddenly, there was an incredibly loud bang and the floor shook and rumbled. We both jumped up, and while Z was putting herself back together, I ran to the window. What I saw was amazing and ominous. A cloud of dust and smoke was spreading from near the town center. We just stared out there and then at each other. She finally broke the silence. "We need to hide. They must have broken through. Let the security team and Dr. Pratte deal with it. Please Enola, for once don't argue with me! I can let them find you." "Who? " I asked, confused as I could be. "Whoever broke through, damn it. Remember, the golden child. If they are here to help we will know soon enough. For now, you can't be exposed to whatever they let in. There is a safe room, and we must try to make it there. Please Enola don't give me that look, just do as I say or everything was for nothing!"

Chapter Seven: The Safe Room

Z grabbed my hand and pulled me into our room. She instructed me to grab enough clothes for a couple of days and to get our hygiene items from the bathroom. I reluctantly did as I was instructed. She was on a mission and did as little speaking as possible. She opened the closet door and dug out two duffle bags I had never seen before. They were full and looked to be quite heavy. She handed me one and pleaded with me to do as she said and be as quiet as possible. I simply nodded and heaved the heavy bag over my shoulders.

I followed Z silently out of our room and down the hall, which led to the main part of the mall store we were living in. The entire storefront was glass windows so we could see that no one was near us at the moment. Z crouched as she opened the front door leading into the center of the mall. She had gone into some kind of Commando mode. She swiftly exited the door and waved for me to follow. She was jogging and half bent over so I did the same. We quickly passed three stores, and she crouched down and pulled me with her. She looked into my eyes to be sure I was paying attention and placed her finger to her lips. I got it. I will be quiet.

Damn, how stupid does she think I am? She crept to the edge of the railing and scanned the bottom floor and escalators. I guess she liked what she saw because she returned to me and motioned for me to follow her again. We crept slowly down the escalator and dashed for a maintenance door. Z keyed in a code to a panel next to the door, and the door popped open slightly. She quickly pushed it open and shut it behind us, once again entering a code into the keypad to the right of the door. The lock engaged with a loud click and lights came on, revealing a corridor that led to another door.

I whispered to her, "Can we speak now? I have so many questions." "Not yet, I'll explain when we are in the room. Move down to the next door. Come on, let's go!" She said, and then we trotted down the long corridors until we arrived at the second locked door. Once again, Z knew the code, opened the door, and locked it behind us. A few steps away were two doors, one on each side, and a dead end. We opened the door on the left and the lights came on automatically. It was just a small office with a desk, chair, and filing cabinet. Z lifted the receiver on the phone that was on the desk and pushed in yet another code.

The desk slid slowly to the right, revealing a staircase descending into the darkness. She grabbed my hand and we started down. As we navigated the steep steps, the desk slid back into place and lights came on. At the bottom of the steps was another corridor that ended at a large metal door. She tapped in another code turned to me and said, "Honey, we are home." When I stepped inside, the inner lights came on, revealing a small room that was almost a mirror image of our bedroom, minus my paintings. It was much smaller though and had a door that led to a bathroom. It also had a fridge and microwave. We dropped our backpacks on the floor and sank into the bean bags.

We were both exhausted from scurrying to this place and the adrenalin rush. Obviously, she had set this up just for us. That answered my questions about how many people were going to hide there. "So, this place is only for us, no one else gets to hide?" "Just us. I have been coming down here to practice the run and give the place a makeover. We had to have a little of our flare. We have everything we need for at least a couple of months. But once the intruders leave, we can go back out." "But how will we know they left? Who are they?" Z told me, "I can only guess at who or what broke in. No one knows. But whoever is left when it is over will come to get us. If no one comes when we get low on supplies, I will go check things out. This has always been a contingency plan since the place was built." Z wiggled herself up from the chair and moved our packs to the corner of the room. She grabbed two bottles of water from the fridge, and as she handed one to me, she began to laugh.

"I forgot we were covered in the paint until just now. You look ridiculous! Let's go get cleaned up and make some food. Then I will answer whatever questions I can, or we could continue what we started upstairs." She winked and smiled at me, then she took a long drink from the water bottle and stripped off her clothes while strolling toward the bathroom. I just looked down at myself and, for the first time since the escape began, I noticed all of the dried paint all over me. I did the same wiggle and stretch maneuver to get up from the bean bag and followed her to the shower. I knew she was trying to distract me from what was happening and from asking questions but what the hell? I needed a shower.

Chapter Eight: Angels and Demons

The doors to the safe room began to shake and squeal. Someone was breaking in. We had been inside here for a week with not a hint of what was going on outside. Zeynep started to pace the room in a panic. "They are coming! I am sure they will remove me first, but then they will want you. Enola, do as they say. Don't be your stubborn pig-headed know-it-all self. Please! I am begging you. They most likely want you kept safe. " I started to ask her what she could possibly be talking about when the door burst open and two very large men stepped in. They were definitely not from New Eden.

They wore strange jumpsuits, and through the faceplate, I could see they had piercings and wild hair. The first one in grabbed Z by her arm and demanded to know her name. I never moved from the beanbag chair I was sitting in. She told them her name and was thrust out of the door into the arms of another man waiting outside. She did not say a word as I heard them escort her up the stairs and out. The man left in the room with me was a strange sight. He was at least six and a half feet tall and very broad-shouldered. He removed his helmet. Half of his face looked like it had melted and slid down a bit. Half of his head had no hair and the skin appeared to be bubbled. Yet, the other side of his face had beautifully chiseled features. He had jet black hair and piercing blue eyes. He was a half-angel and half-demon.

He sneered and said," You must be Enola then. I am Falcon, and you are in my charge. Get up, you now belong to Caesar. It will be easier for your friend if you don't give me any trouble. I know you can hear me little pure one, get the fuck up, my niceness is waning!" I refused to get up from the bean bag I was seated in and ignored him. I even turned my head away in a childish gesture. He thrusted a red biohazard looking jumpsuit at me and demanded that I put it on and go with him. I told him that I was not going anywhere until I spoke with someone in charge of New Eden or my parents, if he could produce them Falcon sneered at me and tilted his head just a fraction. My ignorance of my situation seemed to give him great amusement. "You don't know what you are, do you? The others were told sometime during their entrapment below ground. I guess your people still had hopes for the future and kept you in the dark."

I would not give him the satisfaction of seeing my surprise and confusion. I just glared at him and did not say a word. " You are The Eve. Actually, from what I found in the lab, you are the original where all others came from. I have met three Adams but no other Eve. They all knew who and what they were by the time I met them. They all even know about you. You are essentially their mother after all. Not that any of you actually have biological parents anyway." Frustrated I spat out, " You don't know what you are talking about. I have never had children and I have parents." His grin widened, and he began to laugh, that kind of belly laugh you can't fake.

He laughed so hard he had tears in his eyes. "I can't believe I get to be the one to explain this to you. I really shouldn't, I should let Caesar be the one, but hell, I can't help myself. I hate your kind, you are an abomination and a virus. I am not a scientist, but I can explain the gist of it to you. I'm sure you can use that superior brain of yours to fill in the blanks. Let's start with your companion, Zeynep, is it? She is a genetically manipulated human. Normal start, egg meets sperm, they fall in love and procreate. Only with her type, it is in a lab in a machine, and as soon as DNA strands begin to produce, they are removed and manipulated to what they want the child to be. For an organism to grow and thrive, two separate DNA strands cannot exist. The natural ones are removed as quickly as they are produced and replaced until the organism mutates for survival's sake and starts producing the superior DNA strand or something like that. That is her type, not your type. You following me so far, Pumpkin?"

I continued to glare at him and gave him no response, but inside, I was a mess. Somehow, I knew where he was going with this. I did not want to hear it, but I had to, so I let him continue without a protest. "You, my naive little pure, one had a different start than any other known creature. No egg, no sperm. Your DNA was synthetically created to be perfect. All lab, no love. You are supposed to be one of the super intelligent, athletic, problem-solving Gods to be bred to each other and repopulate the Earth with kind, gentle new humans. No more wars, no more diseases, no criminals, no handicaps. Perfect health, enough logic, and reasoning to understand the everyone must get along to survive. That was their mission. Not to build safe havens for those real humans that did not go along with the gangs and craziness- those that wanted the good life back. No, they said 'fuck them' and did all this for what they called the best of the best only. They left the rest of us to rot. Then the Blast came."

"What Blast?" I interrupted. "Oh sorry, you people call it "The Day the Earth Shook.' It may have only shaken for you, but for the rest of us, it felt like it turned inside out. The few thousand that survived only did so because they were underground in parking shelters or malls. None of which were as deep as this place. See my pretty face?" He turned to give me a full view of his left side. His skin appeared to be melted and twisted over his skull. He had no hair on that side of his head and no ear either. He worked his hand in front of it like a magician and continued, "I did not always look like this. I was salvaging for supplies for my family. We lived as far away from the city as we could and commuted to find food, medicine clothes.

He went on, "Our home was in the woods and hidden from view. We used rainwater from barrels and grew what food we could. I hunted when I could find anything, but the animals were as skinny as we were. Hunting was illegal, but for that matter, so was capturing rainwater and growing your food. Everything had to be shared. I found a hidden door to an underground shelter that seemed to be abandoned, and I climbed down into it to see if there was anything left that we could use. It took me a while to find my way down to the bottom, but I was happy when I got there. It was fully stocked with drinking water and canned food. Whoever had built it had not been back to get it, so I assumed they were dead. No one would just leave that kind of treasure.

He explained more, "I began stuffing my backpack, when suddenly I was violently tossed around as if the shelter was spinning. I landed on my right side as a blistering heat filled the room. It was over as quickly as it began. I was screaming and writhing in pain for what seemed like forever. When I was finally able to stand, I grabbed my backpack and started the long climb to the surface. I figured the place had been booby-trapped and I had set it off. I learned the truth when I emerged from the hidden door. Everything was gone. I mean everything- not even a blade of grass remained as far as the eye could see."

"I forgot my pain and ran home as fast as I could. I could not let myself believe that the devastation was everywhere. It had to be just here, something I tripped. My wife and son would be fine once I got back home. Everything would be okay. I never found home. It was not there- nothing was. As far as I have traveled in the past seven years I have found only twisted metal here and there. No plants, no wood, no plastic. Nothing but warped heavy metal. We located places underground that still had equipment, people, and supplies, and we began traveling together from place to place, only moving when we ran out of supplies. Our numbers grew, which meant more mouths to feed. Nothing grows in the scorched earth."

He went on, "The soil and the water are all contaminated. A few years back, we found a government facility packed with people who do not travel, and they send out scouts to retrieve supplies. The leader calls himself Caesar; he started the community and he and his warriors make all the rules. He is very smart and very scary. But you will meet him soon enough. That is enough history for today, now get up like I asked you to and put on this fucking suit or I will do it for you. I'm done pussyfooting around with you. This whole experience can be easy or it can be torture. That, my dear, is all up to you and your uppity attitude. You are not better than us, you aren't even really human to me. Don't push your luck, Pumpkin. I have my orders to bring you back unharmed and untainted. Orders only go so far. My men will back up whatever I tell them to say, and the people down here could have all been long dead. Who is going to tell Caesar any different? As for all your friends, if you care about them, what happens to them is all on you.

Exasperated, I turned toward him and stated, "I have a lot of questions, with the most important being, how did you find us? At least tell me that and I will go with you." Falcon rolled his eyes and stated, "That part turned out to be very easy once we started looking for you. At first, we questioned the others. Like the other people in the rest of the facilities we entered had done, they refused to cooperate. The unessential workers were tortured to no avail. So, we began looking for you at your home. We found spilled paint with footprints leading out to the mall. We followed the prints and paint smears here. So, thank you Eve, for leaving us the bread crumbs."

"My name is not Eve," I snapped at him. Damn me and my playfulness. If Blaze and I had not gotten into a paint fight, it would have taken them forever to find us. But then, more people would have been hurt. I thrust out my hand, and he shoved the suit at me. I slipped the huge jumpsuit over my clothes and zipped it up the front. Falcon then handed me a helmet. "Really?" I hissed. "We take the maximum precautions with your kind. We can't let you be exposed to anything from the Earth above. When we breached your barriers, contaminants entered with us. That can't be helped. You will be in that suit whenever you are out of sanitized areas." With no further discussion, he shoved me toward the door. I knew I had no choice but to go. They were armed and vicious, and we were not fighters. Maybe if I was cooperative, they would go easier on everyone. At least, that was my hope.

Chapter Nine: First Day of Confinement

Falcon and I emerged from the tunnel leading to the safe room. There were people all over the mall, ransacking the stores. Everything they grabbed, they placed into large plastic totes. The totes were color-coded and were already piled high. It looked like organized chaos to me. Falcon nudged me forward and grunted. I don't think I can ever bring myself to like him. I did not see anyone that I knew, just his people all dressed in khaki jumpsuits. All of them were dirty and tired looking. Falcon wore the same style of clothes, but his were black with an insignia on his shoulder. I had not had a chance to study the insignia in detail yet and probably wouldn't any time soon. Every time he felt I was not walking fast enough, he gave me another shove from behind. Every time I opened my mouth to say something, he just grunted and pushed me again. I was already beginning to hate him. I've never hated anyone before, so it was a strange feeling. It made me feel tingly inside.

    He had obviously gotten the layout of the facility down pat. He pushed me through the mall and out to the corridors leading to the Town Center. We passed people from my facility along the corridors, and they did not even look at us, they just looked at the floor and picked up their pace. Submission so quickly? I wondered what could have been going on while we were in hiding. We had a security team, and we had resources. I have only seen one gun so far, but we did not need guns here. I always assumed we had an armory somewhere in case of events like this. Where was Mr. Thorn? I kept my mouth shut and tried to walk at the quick pace he was forcing on me. I kept reminding myself that he had already tortured innocent people because of me, and I did not want to provoke further violence. Here, behind me, prodding me on was living proof the even after some kind of catastrophic event, people were still assholes. Now our wonderful and peaceful existence was going to end because of their greed.

    We finally arrived at the town square, where my heart dropped. There on the stage were Dr. Pratte, Zeynep, and Father Joe tied to a post and gagged. Z was shaking and crying; her eyes were wide and it was obvious she was terrified. Laying on the floor of the stage just in front of them where they were tied was the body of Mr. Thorn. Even from a hundred yards away,

I knew he was dead. There was so much blood pooling around his head that there was no way he was still alive. Before I could even think, I began to run toward the stage. I am not sure if the noises I heard were coming out of my mouth or just in my head. The bulbus-shaped helmet I was wearing wiggled around as I ran and distorted my hearing. Z was shaking her head at me and her eyes were even wider than before.

Father Joe bowed his head as if in prayer, and Dr. Pratte just watched me with his wrinkled, watery eyes. I ran swiftly and made it to the stage in seconds. I could feel hands attempting to grab me, but I just kept going. The noise was still swirling in my helmet. I bolted onto the stage without any effort at all. My adrenalin had taken over, and everything became clear and almost in slow motion. I scrambled over to Mr. Thorn, still hoping that there was some way to save him. One look at was used to be his handsome face ruined that idea at once. He had no face. It was just a lump of battered flesh, crushed bones, and blood. So much blood. I quickly checked for a pulse and could not locate one.

A second later, I was at Z's side. At this point, Falcon had just reached the stage. As he climbed up onto the stage, I glared at him and freed her from her bonds. He was staring at me, actually, everyone was staring at me very strangely. He stepped over the battered body of Mr. Thorn without appearing to notice him there at all. His eyes never left me. "Do you always move that fast? I could not keep up with you at all." As he spoke, I maneuvered myself in front of Z to protect her. I don't know how I was going to protect her against him and the eighty or so of his people surrounding us, but it was all I could think to do. "You killed Mr. Thorn! Why! Why! Why would you do that?" Falcon placed his hand on his chest, "Me? I did not kill him, well, not with my own hands. He was your head of security, and he had to be the example to the others. There is no resisting us, and there is no escape. This is what happens to those who even think of disobeying us."

He turned to the crowd, "Everyone got that? I am in charge here. What I say goes and everyone will jump when I say jump. No second chances. We have the pure one now. Everyone here will be assigned an area to pack up. We will all work together. We have six weeks max to get this place boxed up and the boxes secured in our containers. After six weeks, the contaminants will begin to affect everything. Trust us, you don't want that to happen. We have completed this same mission eight times with no glitches. Listen, obey, and work hard. We will all get out with the supplies before they are tainted and before anyone gets the contagion." Falcon abruptly turned toward me and grabbed my arm. He lifted up my sleeve and shoved a needle in my arm before I could even react. Lights out.

Chapter Ten: Lava Lamps and Religion

I was awake but had yet to open my eyes. My head felt cloudy and my muscles quivered like wavy bubbles in a lava lamp. As soon as I could form a clear thought, I began a mental self-evaluation. I had a dull headache but aside from that and muscle weakness, I was in no physical pain. I could wiggle my toes and feel every part of my body. My respiration and heartbeat seemed normal, but my eyelids felt as if they weighed a pound each. It took a minute to get them open, but I accomplished the task at hand and looked around to see what I could see. I was lying on a surgical table in a biohazard quarantine chamber. To enter or exit this room, there were two sets of vestibule doors where you were decontaminated. In the last chamber, the biohazard suits were removed and your body was bombarded with ultraviolet lights and anti-bacterial sprays. There were three of these chambers in the facility, and there was no way for me to tell which one I was in. They were all basically identical and located not far from each other in the lab section.

I sat up slowly, actually grabbing my head on each side with both hands to steady it. I felt as if I was spinning. I quickly regained my equilibrium and looked around the room more closely. Some of my personal things were here in the room. There was a pile of bean bags in the far corner with pillows and plush blankets. My treasured purple and green lava lamp sat on a steel table, along with a bible. A small cooling unit was along one wall.

Through the glass doors, I could see it was fully stocked with my favorite beverages and foods. Wondering how long I had been asleep, I scooted to the edge of the table and lowered myself to a standing position on the floor. My muscles were still wobbly, but I was able to maintain my balance. Along the wall to my right were a sink and a prep table. I warbled my way over to it and tried the faucet, and out came clean, cool water ran from the tap. I filled my cupped hands and splashed water on my face then filled my hands again and drank greedily from them. I did not even bother to walk a few feet away to where there were cups plates and utensils. I was dehydrated and hungry. I made my way to the cooling unit, opened one of the doors, and examined the contents.

Suddenly ravenous, I selected some sliced beef, Gouda cheese, and a plate of cut fruit. Again, I did not bother with plates and utensils. I instead stood at the prep counter and gobbled food down. I returned to the cooler and retrieved a container of orange juice. While returning to the table, I drank straight from the bottle. While I began to eat at a more normal rate, I again turned circles in the room, taking in every item in it. The door in the rear led to a small bathroom. All the containment chambers had one.

There was everything I needed to survive but no electronics. No video feed units. No entertainment of any kind. Only a bible and my lava lamp. Not even piped in music. I began to feel woozy again and stumbled back to the cooler and returned the rest of the food I had not consumed and the bottle of juice. Now I remembered why I am out of sorts. That hideous brute Falcon, who killed Mr. Thorn, injected me with something. I have never even taken an aspirin. There is no telling how long the effects would last in my pure system. I made my way to the pile of soft bean bags and pillows and succumbed to the fatigue that seemed to be spreading through my body.

The next time I woke up, the surgical table was gone and there was someone dressed in a biohazard suit in the chamber with me. She was sitting in a chair that had not been there before, and she was writing in a journal. When she noticed that I was awake, she stopped, closed the book, and just stared at me. I was not sure who was supposed to speak first in this type of situation, seeing as this is my first time being drugged and kidnapped, but I decided to speak first anyway. "So, are you just going to sit there mute or can we have some dialogue? This is my first hostage situation so you will have to forgive me if I am not following proper protocol or etiquette."

My captor gave a little smirk and sighed, "He was right, you are a smart ass. I hope you won't be a handful, too. We have provided you with everything from water to a toothbrush- everything you need and comfort items. That is a whole lot more than people have in Top Side. You should be very grateful. If it was up to me, I would keep you drugged until we returned to Olympus. But lucky for you, it is not up to me. My orders are to keep you healthy and out of trouble. I will come at least once a day to check on you. If there is anything you desperately need, you may suggest it, but I can't promise I'll bring it. Do you have any quick questions before I go?"

I debated with myself whether I should get up off of my comfy bed or just ask questions there. I sensed that if I attempted to rise, she may get edgier than she already was. She felt superior above me while I lay vulnerably on the floor. Let her have her misplaced sense of authority. "Well your name would be the first question, and then why am I quarantined, for how long, and why is the only nonessential thing in my room a Bible?" I, of cours,e had a million other questions but those would get me started. This woman was obviously not going to be overly forthcoming and had a lot of animosity toward me already, so I figured I would start slow and simple.

She rose from the chair, folded it into carrying position, and as she began walking to the vestibule door, she said over her shoulder, "Gnasta is my name. You are here so that we can keep you uncontaminated, and you will remain here until we are packed and ready to leave." The Bible, well it is all you will need to know, so read it and decide your place in the world." With that, she stepped to the vestibule door, which opened at once and closed even more quickly behind her. From my spot on the bean bags, I could not see past the door, so I quickly got up and moved in front of the door. It did not open for me. I stood and watched her go through the first cleansing process. The opposite door opened, and she entered the next vestibule. As soon as she did the door closed and she removed the biohazard suit. She was naked and facing away from me. Her hair was so short it must have been cleanly shaved a week ago. Her body had scars scattered down her back and the back of her legs.

She turned toward me as the lights hit her. She might have been beautiful once. Now, she was scarred all over, and her face had a similar burn pattern that I saw on Falcon. On one eye, she wore a patch and she had a rash that looked painful and raw across her chest. Even with all that, she was a small woman and looked delicate until I looked into her eyes. That one part of her told me she was hard and full of rage. But was this rage directed at me, or just in general? I had a sneaking suspicion it was all for me.

A Bible? Why would it be the only thing I need to know? So many questions and no answers. I go to church as it is required of me to do. I have read the Bible, but it is just a book of fables designed to make you think about the consequences of your actions. Do unto others and all that. So many other books have been written about proper behavior. Books about idealisms, religion, and etiquette have been popular over the years since the Bible was pieced together.

I do not understand why people cling to just that one book and ignore so many other prophets and philosophers. To me, it does not make sense to believe in an all-powerful being that loved his creation so very much that he miraculously impregnates one to have his son, then he lets his son be killed by his creations, then he turns his back on them like a child's forgotten outgrown toy and lets evil things happen to innocent people for no fathomable reason. Every once in a while, he almost completely destroys the planet first by cold, then by water, then by volcanos, earthquakes, and tsunamis. What is next? Will the earth suddenly lose gravity or burst into flames? This all-knowing loving and forgiving God seems awfully vindictive and cruel to me. Yet I do truly take comfort in the peace and tranquility of meditation with candles and incense in church, with the choir singing softly while people murmur prayers. So, what was I to do? I sat on my comfy bed and read the Bible again.

Chapter Eleven: Same Thing, Different Day

Gnasta was true to her word, and she came to check on me every day. She restocked the food and drinks in the cooler unit and took out my trash and dirty laundry. For the next ten days after our initial meeting, she never said a word to me or acknowledged me when I spoke. I was going crazy with nothing to do. In the first week, I had read the Bible two times. It did not change; nothing jumped out at me and said, "Aha! This is the answer to everything that has happened and this is your destiny." I begged her for another book, a computer, or some music, but it was like talking to a wall. I worried about Zaynep and everyone else out there in the facility. I hoped that they were following orders and staying out of Falcon's way. Finally, I resorted to mixing flour and fruit juice together to make a crude kind of paint and decorated my walls. For three days, I worked on an undersea mural with my paints and paper mâché. I created coral and plant life for my bright and colorful fish to hide amongst.

On the twelfth day of my hostage crisis, Gnasta finally graced me with speech. "What do you know of the ocean and sea creatures? Is it just from video feeds and books? I have seen all this for real. You captured the true essence of what seeing things underwater is like. There are light distortions and movements. This is just crazy that you could paint something lifelike that you could not possibly have ever experienced. Maybe you were programmed with the information."

I rolled my eyes and said, "I am not a computer. I was not programmed. I am just as human as you. If I was genetically altered, which I do not believe, so what? Thousands of embryos were. No one ever claimed they were not human." She rolled her eyes, "You are a lab rat. You do not have one set of parents like we do. You are not just altered, you were created by blending DNA from different species of creatures; not all if it was human DNA. That way, you can adapt to your environment as lizards do. You can see in the dark, clear far away like felines can do. Some organisms keep information in their DNA, and the next generation knows these things at birth. Did you ever get bored at school because you already knew everything? Tell me, does that sound like a true human? Even miracles in that book there were nothing compared to you. It isn't natural at all. God did not create you, and men should not play God. "

I did not know what to say. I felt like a person. I mean, I look a little different from most people in little ways, but everyone does. Everyone has different skin tones, hair colors, eye color, and body shape. That is all from blending different nationalities and races. What does she know for sure, anyway? All she thinks she knows is the information told to her by people like Falcon. He is definitely not an intellectual at all. I need real, concrete data about my conception and birth. It will all be in our labs. Gnasta stormed out of my living area without removing the trash or laundry. She did not even look back.

Not even an hour later, while I was putting away all of my painting supplies, Falcon and his right-hand man Graven showed up in the decontamination room. I had never seen Graven without his helmet on until now. They were both naked as they entered, having just come through the other chamber. Wow, that was all that was going through my mind. Graven was perfect. He obviously had not been near the surface when the Earth shook. He looked like chiseled marble, all highly defined muscle and graceful as he walked.

I watched them find shirts and sweatpants in the locker and dress. I could not take my eyes off of him. I had thought that Mr. Thorn was beautiful but I now stood corrected. This man appeared to be in his twenties, tall, muscular with honey blond hair and mesmerizing green eyes. He caught me staring, and his face broke out into an amazing smile that even touched his eyes. He was still naked from the waist up and he did a little spin as if to give me a better 360-degree look. Ah. This one has a sense of humor. I could feel my face getting warm. I was truly embarrassed that I was caught unabashedly scanning every inch of his body, but what could I do now but just go with it?

Both men, now dressed appropriately, entered my room. Graven still wore a big, sheepish grin as he nodded at me and said, "So Enola, did you enjoy the view? You are more than welcome to examine me up close and personal at any time." Falcon shot him a glare and replied, "Keep this professional. You know better than to get involved in any way with her." hH turned his attention back to me and continued. "What did you paint this with? You were not given any supplies to do anything with. You are to sit in here with no stimuli except that Bible. Clean this bullshit off of the wall immediately." I still had not taken my eyes off of Graven, who just stood there grinning at me. Falcon turned toward the door and snapped back at him. "See that she gets it all done, then meet me in my office. We have work to do besides babysitting." With that said, he was back in the vestibule and soon gone from sight.

"So, beautiful, how did you manage to make paint and brushes with just what is in this room?" As he spoke he walked up close to me, standing just inches in front of me. I could smell him. He smelled of the decontaminate with an underlying musk. I was so intent on breathing him in that I did not answer him. He cocked his head a little, spread his arms out, and asked, "Would you prefer I get naked again? All you have to do is ask. Come on, loosen up. I do not share Falcon's disposition or dislike of you. I find you absolutely amazing, beautiful, and unique. Come, talk to me for a while."

He took my hand in his and led me over to the small table and chairs. We sat across from each other and both just sat there staring for several minutes before I decided to speak. "Why is everyone so hostile toward me? What have I done to any of them? I don't get it. How can they be so mean and judgmental toward someone they don't know? It does not make any sense." He took my hand in his and as he gently rubbed his thumb across the back of my hand as he explained things to me. "Some people fear what they do not understand. It has always been that way. This is why people like you had alterations that helped make you special. You do not fear as we do. That is why it seems so crazy to you for the way they are acting. They fear you, but I don't. If you would like, I will take over Gnasta's duties. I would really like to spend time with you and get to know you. I'll answer whatever questions that you have. Well, the ones that I know the answers to. And then you can tell me about being you and what it was like to grow up down here. Deal?" I could not help but smile back at him.

He put me at ease, except for the warmth his hand was generating. The softness of his skin and the way he gently rubbed his thumb across my hand was luscious. "Do you know my friend Blaze? Is she okay? When can I see her?" Graven chuckled a little. "Yes, I have spent a lot of time over the past week with her. That is one reason I feel I know you already. She is perfectly fine and being treated well. She asks about you also. I will try to work it out for you to see her. Is it bothering you that I am touching your hand? I apologize, I just have an overwhelming desire to feel your skin. Is that your superpower? You drive men crazy?" I giggled and responded, "Well, I have never had that effect on anyone but you. You see how Falcon acts toward me. He can't even stand to look at me. I am pretty sure that you are just attempting to be charming, but I appreciate it. It is a relief to have someone be nice to me. I have never held hands with anyone but Blaze, so please don't stop. Ask me anything you want to know. Then tomorrow will be my turn. Deal?" He nodded and smiled at me again with that look that made my insides tingle.

His questions were simple and broad. What were my hobbies? Did I go to school? What music did I like? I told him stories of our life here in New Eden and how I always felt kind of left out of daily life here. I explained Mrs. Bryant and her religious rants and Juniper Lee with her ever-changing hair color. I described what it was like the day the earth shook and how we all reacted. I conveniently left out all information about Shane and the day he attacked me. Zeynep and I had not even breached that subject in years. I did, however, tell him about Z and I being more than just best friends. He did not seem surprised at all, so maybe she had already told him.

I told him about the one and only time I had ever been kissed by a man and how the next time I saw him he was lying on the stage beaten to death. By the time I had gotten to that story, we had moved to the floor, and we were on my bean bag couch. He was still holding my hand and sitting so close to me our sides and legs touched. When I got to the part about Mr. Thorn being killed, he let go of my hand, put his arm around me, and pulled me into a hug. He was nuzzling his face in my hair and rubbing his hands down my arm while I finished talking about it. He whispered into my hair, "I am so sorry that you had to see that, Beauty. Don't cry on me now."

I threw my leg over his and sat in his lap. He smiled at me with a surprised look on his face. I wrapped my legs around his waist, put my arms around his shoulders, and buried my face in his neck. "Please, just hold me for a minute Graven. I just need some connection." He wrapped his arms around me and pulled me even closer. The smell of him was all around me. It was intoxicating. He was squeezing me tight and told me to feel safe; he would not let anything happen to me as long as he was there. I felt warm and tingly all over. I pulled back a little and placed my hand on his oh so perfect face. I leaned in and put my face against his forehead and whispered, "Thank you for being so nice to me and holding me like this. I feel so much better now." I wrapped my arms back around him again, moving around to get comfortable again.

A deep low groan escaped from him, and I felt a bulge growing in his sweat pants. This caused an instant reaction from my body also. I arched my back a little, brushing my breasts against him. It was not a conscious thought, just a natural reaction. He moved his hands to my lower back and ground me into him while nuzzling his face alongside mine. It was my turn to groan now. HIs erection hit just right on my clit and sent pleasure all over me. As quickly as it all started, is ended. He let go of my back and placed his hands on either side of my face. He pushed me back a little so we were face to face, about an inch apart and looking into each other's eyes. He ran a thumb over my lips and said with a raspy out of breath voice, "That went downhill fast. I am sorry, I got carried away. That could get me killed really quickly. I told you that you get to me. I want to kiss you Beauty ,can I? Then we have to get up. I can't take much more of this."

I was not so ready to stop and begged, "Kiss me Graven," as I continued to grind myself on his bulge. He pulled my face to kiss and gently brushed his lips on mine. It was more urgent this time. I pushed toward him even harder and opened my mouth to him. He groaned again and thrust his tongue into my mouth. I was still wiggling around on his lap and took his tongue in my lips and began to suck it. We were both grinding and moaning, our breath turning into panting. I wanted to take his shirt off and run my hands over his chiseled chest. I reached my hands down on each side of him and started to tug his shirt up. He grabbed my hands and held them there. Still breathless and pressed together, he then buried his head in my neck. He was trying to slow his breathing and get control of himself.

"Stop. I have to go. I can touch you like this. It is forbidden. I am enjoying it immensely. Don't get me wrong, I want to do this. But this is as far as it goes. No clothes can come off. Just a little playing. Okay? We have to be careful. You don't understand how much trouble I will be in." He lifted his head and leaned in to kiss me again. This time it was gentle, not urgent, and controlled. Then, he pulled back and scooted me off of his lap. He stood up and began pacing around the room.

I climbed out of the bean bags much less gracefully than he did. "I am sorry, I guess I got carried away. We don't even know each other. I just have been so alone and no one has been nice to me. Then you show up looking and smelling like you do. I was overcome. Did you really mean that we could kiss again sometime?" He was turned away from me but slowly turned his head to look back at me. He smiled that gorgeous smile of his and said, "Same time tomorrow good for you?"

With that, he entered the vestibule and the door shut behind him. He removed his clothes with his back still toward me. No prancing and displaying himself this time. He placed the worn garments in the provided bin and exited through the door on the other side. No hesitation, no glancing back, and no wave goodbye. I sighed and sank back into the bean bags. Why did I get so carried away with a man I did not even know? Not just a man, but my captor, my prison guard. I do need someone to talk to but climbing on his lap and riding him like a pony was just crazy.

Shannon Renner

Chapter Twelve: Friends and Lovers

For two weeks, Graven came every day and spent several hours talking to me. He did not force me to remove my mural; instead, he watched me paint the opposite wall. I chose to paint the garden of Eden since we are New Eden and these people say I am Eve. Adam had a very recognizable resemblance to Graven and Eve looked just like Zeynep. Every day when he left, he would kiss me goodbye but so far, we had not jumped all over each other as we had on the first day. It took all my willpower to keep my hands off of him, but I realized that this was not the time or place to get all hormonal. When he got too close or touched me too much, I backed off.

"So, Beauty, you going to ask me the same question that you do every day?" I continued to paint leaves on the tree and said, "Which one?" "About Z. You ask about seeing her every day, and today of all days, you have not brought her up. Which is a shame since she is waiting in the next room. All I have to do is call for her, and she will be brought in." I could hardly believe what he was saying. I had not seen Z in three weeks, not since that day on the stage with Mr. Thorn lying there. I turned to look at him, and he had a big grin on his face.

"Is she out there? Please don't tease me." Graven pushed the intercom button and told whoever was outside to let her in. He looked positively giddy by the time the vestibule door opened. There stood a naked Z, grinning just as boldly as she was standing. She entered the vestibule, and the door shut behind her. She quickly chose clothes from the locker, put them on, and glided through the inner door, which opened on her approach. I dropped my paintbrush and ran to her. We embraced wildly, with both of us crying and talking at the same time. We were both very concerned about each other and how the other had been treated. She kissed me, wiped away my tears, and led me by my hand to the bean bag pile. "Come, let's sit and talk and hold each other." I did as she prompted and as we cuddled together, she looked around my small living quarters. "It looks like you have everything you need. Are you being treated okay? They have been good to you, yes?" The look of concern on her face brought a fresh batch of tears from me. "I am fine. I have every comfort, and for the past two weeks, I have had Graven to talk to for a few hours a day. But, for some reason, they all hate me. What about you? Are you being treated well? What is going on out there?"

Zeynep began the tale of the outside world to me. "No one has been touched since Mr. Thorn. Everyone was given areas to pack up and jobs to perform. They explained to us that they live in one of the underground facilities. They have found seven other facilities and moved all of the survivors, supplies, and information to the first one they discovered. They made the facility safe from contaminants, and the society is thriving. There are twelve other purebloods like you there. Some of the facilities had twins. They all live together with whoever were their companions from home. So, you and I will stay together. There are a few guards there also, but pretty much they stay in their little castle.

Z went on, "The leader calls himself Caesar. He is a genetic scientist who obviously has a God complex. I have heard talk of him being cruel at times, but as I said, society is thriving. We are going to be fine. They are trying to preserve the human race. This is why we were all hidden away in the first place. Just now it is a dire situation. There are less than three thousand people in the facility. Many are old and beyond the ability to bear children. There is no telling who else survived around this continent or any of the others. Now, enough of that mess. I get to come back every day with Graven until we leave. Then we will always be together. Just promise Enola, no matter what, you will always love and trust me. "Will we ever be alone so we can talk and just be us?" I asked her.

" I don't know. Let's just take it as it comes. Look, I brought a video display. Let's watch a movie and giggle and cuddled and just pretend we are back in our room for a while," Z said. I asked her, "With Graven?" Z told me, "Yes, he is our third for the time being. But come on, look at him! We could have been stuck with a lot worse!" She patted the bag next to her and growled, "You want to come to play with us, big boy?"

Graven gave his usually sexy as hell grin and strutted over to us. "I'll sit next to Enola. I see you all the time." With that, we all cuddled together and began watching "Romancing the Stone". Not long into the film, Graven pulled me closer to him with his arm tucked across my shoulder blades. This put his left hand alongside my breast. He began to softly stroke the side of my breast with his thumb. His simple touch sent shivers through me. With Z sitting next to me, it was a little awkward but I did need to tell her that he and I had become a little more than friends. She had a boyfriend before me, and she had been more than friends with Shane. Then, there was Mr. Thorn, and I was up close and personal with that story. Graven was my first relationship other than her. She would be happy for me. I know that much for sure.

I snuggled closer to him, rubbing my face into his neck. He gave a little moan then turned his head toward mine and leaned in for a kiss. Z surprised me placing her head against me and rubbing my back. She began to push my shirt up and put her hand up to undo my bra while Graven and I kissed and pressed against each other. I pulled back from the kiss, and they both lifted my shirt and bra over my head and tossed it to the floor. He looked at my bare breasts like a starving man would look at a gourmet meal. He cupped them both in his hands as I moved onto his lap. His thumbs were running over my nipples making them spring into attention and throbbing. He lowered his head and gently took my nipple between his lips and gave a little tug. We both groaned as I arched my back. Blaze crawled up behind me, straddling his thighs and pressing up against my bareback. I don't know when she lost her shirt, but I felt her bare breasts pressed against me. Graven began kissing up to my throat and neck while Z ground herself against me and messaged my breasts from behind.

She whispered in my ear, "You know you can't have sex yet Enola, but you can play to a point. Once you get to the new community you can do what you want. You can cum, but you can have no intercourse with a man." I was gasping with pleasure as they both kissed, licked, and ran their hands over me. I maneuvered my hands down his torso and untied his sweat pants. His cock was swollen and ready. I pushed the pants down, freeing him from his confinement. I grasped it in my hand, squeezing and rubbing my thumb across the underside of the head. A loud groan escaped his throat.

We were all writhing against one another. Graven rolled us to our sides while Blaze tugged my sweat pants off. We were kissing and groping, all three panting and hot with desire. They pushed me onto my back, both kissing me and running their hands over me. I had his penis in my left hand moving up and down with the rhythm of his movements. With my right hand, I slid down into Blaze's black panties. Her crease was soaking wet and that made me arch and pant more. They both moved a hand down to my clit, and I immediately spread my legs apart a little further.

Sheer ecstasy overcame me. Graven began to shake and moan loudly, then warm fluid flowed from him onto my hand and hip. His body shuttered. He nuzzled his head in my neck. Z and I were still fiddling with each other. When I realized he was spent, I turned to face her. She pushed me back onto my back and began kissing her way down. Starting at my breasts, she licked, sucked, and nibbled until she reached my clit. She looked up at me, smiled, licked her lips, and then began to drive me crazy. Her soft, full lips brushed my lower lips as her tongue was flicking back and forth. I raised myself as far as I could to watch and push against her. I needed more.

I needed something.. I heard a slight groan next to me and turned to look a Graven. He was renewed. Sitting up cross-legged next to me, he had his throbbing cock in his hand and was pleasuring himself as he intently watched Z perform magic with her tongue.

"Do you want any help with that?" I purred at him. His eyes were full of lust. Z stopped her magic and looked up at him. "You should taste this too." He and I both moaned in response to her tease. She got up and switched places. His face was muscular and a little prickly from his last shave. It was a big contrast to her softness, but it was just as pleasurable. He dug in with more vigor and more passion. As he did his work on me, she straddled my face and I reached up, gripped her hips, and pulled her soaking wet pussy down to my waiting mouth. She moved on top of me while I imitated what was being done to me by Graven. All three of us were grunting and moaning with pleasure. My body started to quiver as I moaned and arched. A sudden wave of pleasure shot through me, all the while my tongue and fingers were inside of Z. She found her release a few moments after I did.

We all detangled ourselves and lay panting. Ah. This is what I had been missing. Graven and Z had not touched each other at all. It was all about me. I did not have to breach the subject of Graven possibly being my boyfriend, as it seems it is already known to them both. I felt fulfilled and happy. I could have danced a jig right there. Graven crawled over to me and took me in his arms. "Did you like it?" I kissed him deeply and tasted my juices on his lips. I guess he could taste Zaynep on mine. I did not care. I just wanted the feeling of him wanting me, with his arms around me, his mouth on, mine and our naked bodies sliding all over each other. I wanted to feel that rush again right now. I grabbed his cock and rubbed it against my clit. "Fuck me, Graven." He pulled back from me and pushed my hand off of his penis. "Whoa now, missy. Don't get crazy on me. We did what we can get away with. We will do it again, just not right now. We need to leave soon and it would be best if we showered first." Z took my hand and pulled me up. "Us first." With that, we were walking toward the bathroom together.

Once inside the bathroom with the door shut between us and Graven, she whispered to me, "There are things we need to talk about, but everything in your room is recorded. Yes, my love, even what we just did. I am fine, and we will be fine. Don't worry. Now get in there, and I will wash your back, and if you're sweet, I'll rub the front some, too." We both giggled and stepped into the shower. The water was hot, and we took advantage of the perfumed soaps they had provided for me. The steam took on the smell of jasmine and lemongrass. Z pulled me to her and rubbed her thumb over my bottom lip. Then she sucked that lip in her mouth. We both reached down and began fondling each other.

I was a little sore, but the ache added to the experience. Z broke the contact, gave her best smile, and began washing her hair. I did the same thing, all the while watching the bubbles run down her breasts along her abdominal muscles and straight to her crotch. I could still taste her. I pulled my thoughts away from the pleasure I wanted to give her and receive in return, and I rinsed my hair out. We dried each other off with soft, fluffy, purple towels. I was more at ease than I had been since the invasion.

Graven took a lot less time in the shower. He came out naked and glistening. My, was he a fine specimen. He gave me a lingering kiss goodbye, and they both stepped into the vestibule. They deposited their soiled clothes in the bin, and the other door opened. Graven glanced back at me and smiled. Then, they were gone. Z had forgotten to take her video display chip with her. Thank God. Now I had something to keep my mind off of being locked up alone.

Chapter Thirteen: A Little Surprise"

I was patiently awaiting the arrival of my best friend and boyfriend. I was lounging on the bed, wearing very little. I had the video display showing my favorite Bogie movie, "To Have and Have Not," on the wall. The vestibule door opened, but instead of who I expected, Falcon entered. There he was, naked and carrying bags. I had to admit that even with his scars he was almost as luscious as Graven. He would probably be more handsome if he ever smiled. He always looked sad and angry at the same time.

I did not bother to get up or cover up, and I returned my attention to my movie. Falcon stepped through the door and placed the bags on the counter. He pulled out a pair of sweatpants and put them on. He walked over and said, "Where did you get that? They smuggle it in for you?" I hushed him, "This is my favorite line in the movie." Just then the old man asked, "You ever been bit by a dead bee?" I giggled and turned my attention back to Falcon. "Sit, please. Finish watching this with me then you can scold me or whatever you came to do." Surprisingly, he plopped down beside me and quietly watched the movie. He did not touch me and never said a word until it was over.

"I never saw that movie before. I have not seen many movies at all. Keep the display on, and come see what I brought you." He stood up and walked to the kitchen area, and I followed close behind. As I stood next to him, he began taking items out of the bag and placing them on the counter. I could not help but notice how great he smelled and even leaned in a little closer to get a better whiff. He kind of smelled like bay leaves and rosemary. I wanted to touch his chest and see if his skin was as taut and silky as Graven's, but I controlled myself. This was my jailer. He had Mr. Thorn killed. He is not my friend, no matter how handsome and aromatic he may be.

"I brought you some art supplies so you can stop defacing the walls. I also heard you like to cook so I found your supplies in your old room and brought them also. I thought maybe we could cook lunch together. I used to like to cook for my family when we found food. Do you mind?" He never even looked at me, he just continued unpacking things. He had even brought my hand mixer. I had to admit it was a surprise, and I did love to cook. Itarted putting the supplies away and left out only what I need to make a soufflé. He surveyed what I had chosen to leave out and what I was removing from the cooling unit. "Is it to be a soufflé then? Just tell me what you need me to do, and I will get to work." I think he almost smiled. Falcon chopped the onion and garlic while I sautéed the sausage. We worked together well and soon had a Brie, pear, and sausage soufflé in the oven.

I set the small table while he expertly threw together a tossed salad. By the time I brewed some raspberry tea, the meal was ready to be placed on the table. I had been so caught up in the joy of cooking and watching him act human for once I forgot all about the fact that I was only wearing purple lace panties and a skimpy tank top. I also forgot that the reason for me being dressed this way was because I was expecting my boyfriend and wanted to wow him. He was late and here I was dressed like this getting ready to have lunch with Falcon. "I forgot I was not properly dressed. Sorry. Let me put on something less comfortable." Falcon looked me over, "That would be for the best, I think. I'll get my shirt also. I did not notice we were cooking half-clothed. It has been so long since I had a peaceful moment."

Properly dressed for lunch, we sat across from each other and tasted our creation. The salad dressing he had whipped up with odds and ends from the kitchen was amazing. It had hints of citrus with sweet peanut oil. "You will have to tell me what you put in this dressing. The flavor combination is to die for." He did not answer me, he just kept eating. He seemed to be savoring each bite. Occasionally, I would catch him looking at me. The conversation was sparse and mundane. When we had finished our meal, he gathered the dishes and washed them. I dried and put them away. We chatted about cooking and cleaning duties but nothing important or personal. After the clean up, he seemed to be preparing to leave and I found myself wanting him to stay. I wanted to find out more about him and find a way to make him truly smile.

"Are you leaving so soon? I thought maybe we could talk some more before you go. I know nothing about you." He looked at me with those sad and angry eyes and said," I know a lot about you, Enola. I am required to watch you 24 hours a day. I obviously can't be awake that long so your life is on tape. I watch you cook, paint while singing, and pace around talking to yourself. I watch your interactions with Gnasta, Graven, and Zeynep. I find myself thinking of you as a victim of the scientists, when for years before I met you, I imagined you as a devil. I wish to know you better and feel protective of you somehow. But I can't feel any of those things. You are different from the other Pure Bloods, but I have a job. My job saves lives in the end. I fancy myself a modern-day Robin Hood. I seek out what we need to survive and take it by any means possible back to the people. I would protect you if I could. I can't even protect you from yourself, though. I have to go now. "

He began to walk toward the door. I placed my hand on his arm and stopped him. "Do you watch everything? " He nodded but did not look at me. "Do you like what you see, Falcon? What do you think of me? I imagine being with you. Even your scars have a beauty to them. But I am with Graven, and I would not do anything to hurt him." He abruptly turned to look at me. "You believe that you and Graven are exclusively together. I can tell that. Things are not always as they appear, my dear. After we get back to base, you will never see either of us again. I wish he would have told you that. He has his purpose being with you. I have already said too much." He stomped off to the door and entered the vestibule. Once inside, he stripped off his clothes and placed them in the bin. He never looked back. I knew he would be watching me later and that gave me pleasure. My friends did not visit me that day, so I sifted through the items that Falcon brought me. I chose a piece of canvas and began to draw a portrait of him as a naked warrior fighting his demons.

It was after eight in the evening when I finished the portrait. I placed it where I knew he would see it on film. All of the time I was painting, I was thinking of the things he had said. What was Graven's purpose for being with me? Why would I never see them again if I was to live like royalty? What is it that he seemed desperate to protect me from but feels obligated to let happen to me? My life, which had seemed so normal and mundane, had become one big question mark.

I prepared a salad for dinner using the rest of his delicious dressing. As I ate, I raised my fork in salute to him. That made me giggle, and I found myself hoping he found it amusing too. Was he watching me live now or would he see this later? I decided that he probably always watched live except for when I slept, which was basically the same time every day. After cleaning the dishes and putting everything away, I decided to play with him. I sashayed across the floor with exaggerated hip movements while slowly taking my clothes off.

I stood naked in the middle of the room and began to dance to the music in my head. I picked a song and sang it low and deep while slow dancing and running my hands over my body. I realized how stupid I must look and stopped. I was not Zeynep. I went to the bathroom for a shower, put on my favorite sweats, and climbed in bed. It was Bogie time again. I fell asleep to the sounds of the African Queen.

Chapter Fourteen:
Last Days in the Fortress

For the next week, I spent a few hours a day with Falcon. Sometimes we talked, and other times we cooked or watched movies. Graven and Z only came to visit twice. We did what we usually did and spent little time talking. I was very content, for being held captive, I mean. I was able to see my best friend, I had my first ever boyfriend, and he was attentive and loving toward me. I also had Falcon. He was still a mystery to me. I guess he is my friend, but he is in charge here and is holding me captive. He had Mr. Thorn killed. My feelings for Falcon are hard to pin down. Though I am very sexually attracted to him and have made that clear, he has never made any advances toward me. I tease him but I would never betray Graven's trust. Maybe it is the same with Falcon. He and Graven are friends and work together, and he knows we are together. I think I will ask him about it to satisfy my curiosity.

I was painting a picture of Falcon when I realized that it was getting late in the day. He always visited me in the afternoon, and it was well past four o'clock. Where was he? He had not missed a day in over a week. This unexpected absence made me realize how much I looked forward to the time we spent together. I was trying to think of what I could have done or said that scared him away when I heard the outer vestibule door open. My heartbeat quickened just a little and a smile spread across my face as he walked naked into the vestibule. He had a few bags with him again. I watched with admiration as he selected sweatpants and a t-shirt from the cabinet and walked toward me. Graven was physically perfect, but there was just something about Falcon that gave him an advantage somehow.

"You look actually happy to see me today." I smiled even broader, "Why have you kept me waiting all day? I was beginning to think you weren't coming." He was bending over to place the bags on the floor. As he stood back up, I embarrassed him, burying my head in his chest with my arms wrapped around him. "Don't leave me here alone Falcon. I've been locked up for weeks, and I am getting very stir crazy. Can't you understand that? I have never been alone until you locked me in here. Not ever."

He pulled away from my grip and smiled at me. "Come on, let's see what I brought you today. We will be leaving New Eden in a few days and I did not want you to have to leave behind any of your things. Blaze and I packed up what we could of your personal belongings. They have been disinfected, and everything in this room now can go with us when we leave. I have been very busy all day and I have not eaten anything since the lunch we had together yesterday. When you are ready, will you cook something for me? Anything you want. I am not picky." I did not bother going through the bags, I could do that when he was not here. "I am famished also. I assumed you would be coming for lunch so I waited. Tell me how things are going with all the moving and packing out there while I make us something to eat," I told him.

I walked over to the kitchen and peered into the cooler. I was trying to decide what we should have for dinner when he said, "Maybe you should change your clothes. You are covered in paint." Seizing my opportunity to ask about why he never touched me, I looked down at my attire and giggled. I took a step closer to him and pulled my shirt over my head. I handed it to him, placed my hand on his arm for balance, and reached down and removed my shorts.

There I was, inches from him in nothing but a skimpy, lacy bra and panties. He handed my clothes back to me and walked past me to the cooler. He reached in and removed some carbonated water, drinking the entire thing in one gulp. "You don't like how I look? Or is it that you respect my relationship with Graven? I would never cheat on him, you know. I am just playing with you." Falcon turned toward me with a strange look on his face. He walked over to my table and sat down without a word. He looked worried or confused. I could not tell. I forgot all about attempting to look sexy and tease him. I sat down at the table also. "What is wrong? You look worried. Was it something I said?"

Falcon looked at me with sadness in his eyes. "Enola, hear me out. Okay? We are leaving in a few days so this would all be clear to you then anyway. I don't want to be the one to tell you, but I can't watch you believe something that is not true. Graven is not your boyfriend. He has many other women in his life. He has a pretty-boy job. His goal was to get you ready for when we get back to home base. He and Zaynep live together with Gnasta. They are all three together every night in the same bed. I am sure he loves the time he spends with you, but it is not exclusive, and he knows once we get home he can never touch you again. He should have explained things to you instead of leading you to believe that there was more than just something physical going on. I know you don't want to believe me and you want to be mad at me and blame me, but I have never lied to you. I can show you proof if you need to see it."

I was shaking my head during his entire speech. It could not be true. Neither Z nor Graven would betray me, but maybe they don't see it as a betrayal. "Show me then." Falcon logged in to the wall computer and brought up the camera system. He pressed the keys in to bring up the camera in the room that Graven was assigned to. There in that room were Z and Gnasta practically naked and dancing around the kitchen. There was no sound but it was obvious that they were listening to music while preparing dinner. We watched them for twenty minutes while they continued their chores while dancing and every time they passed each other they touched or kissed, like sZ and I always do.

Graven came into view from another room wearing only a pair of shorts. He greeted each of the women by pulling their hair and arching their necks back while he licked their chests. It was obvious that they were all very comfortable with each other. Falcon was telling the truth. "Turn it off please. I have seen enough." "I did not want to upset you. I just did not want a scene later." "I am not upset. I have no right to be. They never lied to me; they just failed to mention things they knew I would not like. I have always known how promiscuous Z is, I just wish I had known they were living together. So, what should we make for dinner "

Falcon looked surprised, but he stood up and walked to the cooler, peering inside at the contents. Over his shoulder he said, "You might think about that change of clothes now. I need to concentrate on cooking and not set the place on fire." I would have normally pranced around and teased him, but I did feel a little loss from my new information, so I did as he asked. I even put on pants and a long sleeve shirt. Everything was covered. When I returned to the kitchen, he had all the fixings out to make pasta primavera.

We spent the next hour chopping veggies and talking about our favorite ways to eat each of them. The conversation always flowed smoothly between us. Falcon whipped up some more delicious salad dressing, and I placed some garlic rolls in the oven. By the time we set the table, the pasta was al dente. "All we need is a bottle of white wine," he teased. "Do you have alcohol in your facility? It was not allowed here. No drugs, no alcohol, no tobacco, I told him. "No. We don't. Just wishful thinking. All of those things were outlawed top side years before the destruction of everything. You could get them in back alleys and basements sometimes," he told me.

"We wanted to try to make some whiskey in the main base, but Caesar forbids it. He was in the conglomerate, you know? He has a vision far beyond the original ideas for these hidden facilities. He runs a tight ship, and he will not let anyone disobey his rules. He can be quite cruel. But you will see soon enough," Falcon told me.

Dinner was delicious and for the rest of the meal, we talked about music and art. As always, he steered the conversation away from himself. It was all questions about me, what I can do, and what I like. Whenever I tried to learn more about him, he evaded the questions. Whenever I asked questions about "The Day the Earth Shook," he said I had to wait untilwe got to the facility. All he told me was that in Top Side they referred to that day as "The Cleaning."

Once the leftovers and freshly washed and dried dishes were put away, he started to say his goodbyes. "Don't leave yet. It is early, let's watch a movie or play a game. I don't want to be alone anymore Falcon. Please." "Only if we can watch something funny. I am not in the mood for those action films you like so much." I broke out the most fabulous grin, and I was actually clapping my hands and jumping around. "I have the perfect movie! It was banned centuries ago for being so over the top offensive. I'll cue it up." He sat down on my pile of fluff, and I sat next to him hugging a pillow. Immediately on the wall across from us began the movie "Blazing Saddles." I was worried that he may be one of those who would find it offensive, but he smiled a couple of times, and then the most amazing thing happened.

Falcon laughed! The more he laughed, the more I did. He looked much younger when laughing. I leaned into him, and he put his arm around me. We finished the movie like that. I did not want the evening to end yet, so I quickly started another funny movie. This one was not so offensive, it's called "Arsenic and Old Lace." Falcon did not protest like I thought he would; instead, he snuggled even deeper into the pillows and pulled me a little closer. I have no clue as to what point I fell asleep or for that matter, when he did. I awoke in the dark and looked around. My eyes do not require an adjustment period as some people's do.

We were both asleep, and he was snuggled up behind me. I did not move for fear of waking him and causing him to leave. I was back asleep in seconds. An hour or so later, I felt him climb out of bed. He was being so careful not to wake me up so I pretended to be asleep. The vestibule door opened then closed behind him. I remained still so he would think he got away without waking me. I was a little disappointed that he left. It would have been nice to wake up in his arms. That would be a normal life- a normal relationship for a normal person. I was beginning to fear that nothing was ever going to be normal for me and that it was never intended to be that way. I would just have to make the best of what I am given. There is no sense in ever being depressed or stressing over things you cannot control.

Chapter Fifteen: One for the Road

I did not see anyone for two days after Falcon snuck out in the middle of the night. Even Gnasta did not come to remove the trash or dirty clothes. I felt entombed. What if they left and did not take me? I guess I would just have to figure a way out of here. I could get out. I did not doubt that. I could do just about anything I put my mind to, and if these intruders were correct I was genetically designed that way. I would make myself a proper cup of Earl Grey and some breakfast. It felt like a quiche kind of day. I had plenty of fresh veggies, cream, and eggs.

While sipping my tea, I made a puff pastry crust and whipped the eggs and cream with thyme and rosemary. A half an hour later, I popped the quiche in the oven and sat down with another cup of tea. The aromas of baking cheese and spices filled my little home, and I forgot all about being left behind. I enjoyed cooking and enjoyed eating even more. Z always makes remarks about how enthusiastic I was about food. She made me go to the gym a lot, but in truth, I did not need it. I never gained any weight, no matter what I ate or drank. I have always been the same relative size. Not skinny by all means but not buff and long-limbed like Z. Maybe it is part of my design. I don't know. I want to look at my files

The quiche was almost ready, so I was dicing up from fruit as my side dish. The yogurt and granola were already ready to top it. I heard the outer door begin to open. I decided not to act excited or even turn to look who was coming in. As I removed my breakfast from the oven, the inner door opened. I placed the quiche on the table and sat down to enjoy my meal. Falcon, Z, Graven, and Gnasta all entered my kitchen and stood around my table. "Grab some plates, there is enough for you all to eat as well. There is granola yogurt and shaved coconut on the first shelf." Graven kissed me on the cheek, "Great! I am hungry, and it smells amazing!" Falcon and Gnasta loaded up plates and sat without saying a word. Zeynep sauntered over and hugged me, "I have missed your wonderful quiches. Yum!" and then she sat down also.

"So, once we finally get to the settlement, what happens to me?" I asked. Falcon put his fork down and lowered his head a little. "You will be taken to the tower where the rest of your kind live. Zeynep will live one floor down with the other companions. You most likely will never see the rest of us again." Enola rolled her eyes, "My kind! I hate when you act like I'm some kind of subspecies!" Falcon reached over and gently took her hand.

He told Enola, "You have eight base gene nucleotides. That is crazy and does not exist in nature just like a human giving off so many pheromones. You are something else entirely. Not a subspecies, an advanced species. Your eyes adjust to the light as swiftly and efficiently as a cat, your skin keeps itself moist to control your body temperature in any climate. You are immune to disease and will live three times as long as a normal person. That is just some of the list, my dear. In time they will learn a lot more about you and be able to tweak your children's genes and DNA to be even better. You are the beginning of better, stronger humans that will repopulate the earth. "

Enola stood from the table and walked to the cooling unit. "So, I have what? Two or three kids in my life and that is going to do all of this? Not possible! Who crazy idea was all this anyway?" Falcon took a deep breath, looked her in the eye and said,"Your parents. We leave tomorrow, sweetheart, so I need you to be ready. Pack up only what you have to have with you. We will be living in a container on the back of a truck for a few weeks. There will not be much room, no privacy at all. We will all be together till we arrive at the settlement. I'd like to stay here with you tonight if that is okay with you." Enola nodded her head in response and returned to the table. The rest of the meal was consumed in utter silence. Enola felt the others staring at her from time to time but she ignored it. When the meal was finished, Z helped Enola clear the table and do the dishes. The conversation was about the tasks at hand only. When they finished, everyone left and Enola began to paint. She thought that maybe she should feel scared or upset, but she had never had much negative emotion in her life and when she did it, was gone as quickly as it had arrived.

The afternoon passed as quickly as it always did when she threw herself into a project. By the time her stomach started growling and alerted her to the fact that she skipped lunch, it was already time for dinner. She opened the cooling unit to see what she should cook since it was her last night here. Steaks! She would grill steaks with mushroom, onion, red pepper, and asparagus. Maybe she would make a hollandaise sauce and a salad. Enola began to make a garlic lime marinade for the steaks. She took out two in case Falcon showed up for dinner. She wanted him to come back. She felt safe in his company, and he made her giggle a lot. Who would have thought that in just a few weeks she could go from hating him to looking forward to his company?

She took out the best dishes she had in her little prison cell and set the table as if for a formal affair. The setting looked lovely with the centerpiece she made out of colorful empty bottles tied with ribbons from one of her shirts. It was amazing how she could make art out of scraps. Enola turned on her music program, and violin music emanated from the speakers at once. She wanted her last night, hopefully *their* last night, here to be perfect. She was hoping that Falcon would have sex with her, and they could spend this night pressing their naked bodies against each other, caressing, kissing, and sucking. Just thinking about it made her moist with anticipation. She was slowly rocking to the classical music and preparing the salad when she heard the outer vestibule door open. Her heart picked up a beat, and she put a little more sashay in hip motions.

Falcon watched her on the video screen beginning to prepare dinner. She was dressed in her painting outfit and had bits of paint in her hair. Her overalls were too large and her shirt too small. She was not wearing a bra, and her large, pert breasts were bouncing along as she swayed to the music. She was wearing a white thin cotton top and bright orange thong underwear which were barely covered by the sagging overalls. She looked so incredibly sexy he thought about not going to dinner with her. It was getting harder and harder to resist her. He told himself it was the pheromones she secreted and not her smile and beauty. Falcon sighed as he watched her set the table for two. This would be the last night of good food, music, and movies for him. The ride back home would be crowded and long. Once there, he would hand her over to Caesar and it would be done. He would be greatly rewarded and be allowed his choice of women, weapons, and lodging. Tonight, though, he would have an excellent meal with beautiful company in a civilized atmosphere. He just needed to keep his hands off of her.

Falcon walked through the vestibule door wearing the usual T-shirt and sweatpants ensemble they provided for her visitors. He was also wearing that cocky crooked smile of his. "Honey, I'm home," he called out. I giggled and continued prepping the salad while he sauntered over and kissed me on the cheek. His left hand rested on my bare hip as he did this, sending a shiver of pleasure through me. I turned to face him and purred, "Well that is new?" and stood on my tiptoes and tried to kiss him. Now, both hands were on my bare hips while he kept me at a distance. I pouted as he shook his head. "Oh don't go and get carried away, I was just being cute," I sighed, "Well, I can always hope you want to play house on our last night. I know I do, I really, really do!" He gave me a little shove to create some distance and took over making the salad. "I'll finish this while you go get cleaned up and change. You are covered in paint. Take your time. I will finish making dinner." I scrunched up my face at him and stuck out my tongue. While I walked to the bathroom to shower I said, "You've been watching me on the monitor again haven't you? Well, then I will leave the door open in case you want to watch some more." I saw his posture stiffen a little at my comment, but he did not reply and just went about his work.

With the door open, I tossed my soiled shirt out the door and began to shimmy out of my overalls. Clad only in my bright orange lace thong, I leaned out of the door, "I'd like my steak rare, please." He glanced over his shoulder at me and tried to suppress his surprised reaction, "Two rare steaks coming up." He turned back to the sink and that was it. I was disappointed that the sight of me like that did not stir more reaction from him, but the night was still young.

I took my shower with the bathroom door still open and used my jasmine body wash and my sage and lemongrass shampoo. The aroma filled my living quarters and mingled with the scents coming from the searing steaks. My clothes were on a small shelf outside of the bathroom door. I exited the bathroom with a towel wrapped around my hair and a smaller towel held across my chest, leaving my entire backside exposed. "Smells incredible," I chirped as I turned toward the shelf and began rummaging for clothes. I heard him make a groaning kind of noise and catching his breath. This made me smile and my chest swell.

I dropped the towel on the floor and chose a large, pale yellow half-shirt from the shelf and pulled it over my toweled head. One side hung low on my arm, exposing my bare shoulder. The shirt was very thin and my nipples were very visible. I selected a short denim skirt that barely covered my ass and stepped into it. Dressed now, I scooped up my dirty clothes and put them in the hamper. I walked over to Falcon, bent at the waist toward him, and asked him to dry my hair for me. He gently unwrapped my hair and rubbed it with the towel. It felt very nice to have him gently rubbing my head, and I made a little sound of contentment in the back of my throat. He quickly stopped caressing my hair with the towel and took a slight step back. I stood up straight with my damp hair hanging across my face looking at him through my dangling curls. He reached out his hand toward me, passing the towel back to me. Nothing was said between us, but I could tell by his rigid posture and the look on his face that I was getting to him. This was the last night that we could be alone, and I wanted to spend it rolling around naked with him. I wanted to feel his breath on my skin and lick the sweat from his.

The more I imagined what we could be doing, the hotter I got and the more determined I was to make it happen. He turned back toward the stove and resumed cooking. I was consumed by a different kind of hunger at this point. I knew he wanted me also, and for the life of me, I could not figure out why he was resisting it. The T-shirt he was wearing hugged every one of his tight muscles and accentuated his slim waist. I walked up behind him and wrapped my arms around him, snuggling my face into the center of his back. Falcon took a deep breath and exhaled dramatically. "You are going to make this evening as hard as possible, aren't you?" I giggled and replied, "The plan is to make you as hard as possible as many times as possible. This is our last ever chance to be alone, according to you. I don't know how you feel about me emotionally, but I know you have a physical reaction." I slid my hand down from his chest to the bulge in his pants and lightly ran my fingers over it. I ground my body into him as I tightened my grip on him. Another dramatic sigh escaped his lips, but he did not push me away. In fact, he led back into me a little bit. Falcon turned off the stove and turned to face me.

There was a fire in his eyes I have never seen before. "Why should I get involved with you knowing it would be just this one night? I have come to care about you and yes, it is obvious I want you, but why would I act on it knowing you can never be mine? I have women, whores I use when needed, but I have never cared about another woman since my wife died. I don't let myself care or get involved. But I care about you Enola, I don't want to get any more involved than I already am just to lose you too. I want you, I do. I want to feel your tongue in my mouth. I want to caress every inch of you." He rubbed his thumb gently across my nipple as he spoke to me. I don't think he even realized he was doing it. My nipple instantly became so hard, and I tingled down to my knees. I pressed closer to him and cupped his chiseled jaw in my hands. "Kiss me, Falcon. Let's think of now, tomorrow may never come. Kiss me please, I need you." I was almost panting as I spoke. He leaned down and gently touched his lips to mine. I squeezed his face in my hands and thrust my tongue into his waiting mouth.

What started as a gentle kiss turned hard with need. He lifted me up slightly, and I wrapped my legs around his waist. He took two steps toward the table and sat me down on the edge. I tugged his shirt over his head and ran my hands all over his bare chest. He leaned in and gently kissed my forehead and then my eyes, nose, lips, and, finally, moved to my neck. He was gently kissing, licking, and sucking. I moaned with pleasure while my hands returned to the even harder bulge below. He gently pushed my hands away. "No," he groaned. "I'm going to come way too fast if you start touching me now. Let me play first." The grin on his face made the scarred side look evil, but it made me moist with anticipation. I was not wearing any panties and barely wearing a skirt. He pushed my thighs a little wider apart and slid his finger inside of me. I threw my head back and cried out, but he smothered my sounds with his lips and tongue.

With fingers inside me, he massaged my clit with his thumb. He lifted my shirt with his other hand and bent me back toward the table and sucked my nipple into his mouth. Licking, sucking, and pulling on my nipple with fingers pumping inside me and thumb flicking, I was going crazy with need. I began to squirm and rock against him mumbling, "Please, please." Then it happened all at once. The release of an incredible orgasm that I felt over my entire body. Everything tingled, and I was visibly shaking. He let my nipple fall from his mouth and I collapsed on the table, panting. "More," was all I could say, and he accommodated me. He pushed my thighs onto his shoulders and began kissing my thighs toward the center of my pleasure. He cupped my cheeks in his hand and pulled me into his face where he buried his tongue inside me. He was pulling me into him while twirling and thrusting his tongue. It was too much too soon, and I started to squirm. There was no slow build up to a release. I just exploded again.

Screaming out his name, I thrust myself up, rubbing my lips all over his face. It was almost as good as the orgasm I had three minutes earlier. The thought made me giggle. He lowered me back to the table where I wrapped my legs around his waist once more. My arms slid around his neck, and we began to devour each other's faces again. I could taste my pleasure all over him, and it brought me right back to a throbbing need for him. He pulled back just a little and whispered, "What else do you need from me?" That caused another groan to escape my lips. "I want you to do to me whatever you want. Anything that will please you. I want you inside me, Falcon. Fuck me, please." He smiled a big, beautiful smile, but his eyes looked sad. He walked, carrying me to the pillows, and set me down there.

He pulled my clothes off gently and just cuddled, kissed, and caressed me. I knew he could not be inside me the way we wanted but I wanted him to know I would do it for him. I ran my hands all over him and tugged his sweat pants off. The sight of his erect penis sent fresh chills all over me. "Is that for me?" I purred. He groaned as I slowly kissed my way down his chest while keeping a firm grip on my prize. I was surprised to discover that he was clean-shaven down there. As I stroked his throbbing cock, I sucked his balls into my mouth while twirling my tongue around them. He moaned even louder and began to squirm as I had done before. I was afraid he would cum before I had the chance to taste him, so I exchanged his scrotum for his cock and began to suck and lick my way down it while stroking the shaft. I kept his balls cupped in my other hand and squeezed them. He seemed to like it so I squeezed harder and moved my finger around his anus at the same time. He was mumbling something that I could not make out, but it sounded like he was enjoying my efforts and his enjoyment flamed my passion. I moved my body to where I was lying down his leg. It gave me better access to play with his ass and rub my clit on his leg.

I continued to stroke and suck while massaging all around and rubbing myself on him. He began to quiver and jolt then exploded on my tongue. The feel and the warmth of it, along with his shin rubbing me made me cum again also. I continued to suck on him. I wanted more, but he started to laugh and pulled me up on top of him. "I am not as young as Graven, I'll need a few minutes or so before I will be of any use to you." He rolled us on to our sides and began to kiss me, gently this time. Even without the urgency, the kisses were passionate and breathtaking. We were lying there for hours kissing, caressing, and fondling. It felt like forever yet ended too soon.

Chapter Sixteen:
Time to Hit the Yellow Brick Road

The monitor on the wall chirped and then a voice told us that we should prepare to leave. I wanted to stay longer, wrapped in his strong arms and feeling his breath on my skin, but the time had come that I had been dreading yet was also very curious about. Today, I begin a new chapter in my life, a life out of New Eden and through the scorched lands to another underground facility filled with survivors and other people like us and me.

Falcon struggled up and out of our pile of pillows and walked with purpose to the bathroom. He shut the door, and I could hear water running. There was no last kiss or parting sentiment from him; he was just back to his rigid stance and all business. I don't know what I expected or why it made me a little sad. Part of me wanted him for my own, wanted him as my partner so that no one else could have him. I knew deep down that with my hormonal tendencies, I could not be monogynous but I could fantasize about it. As quickly as the thought of sadness hit me, it was gone.

The excitement of a new journey took over, and I tidied up the kitchen and had everything ready when he exited the bathroom dressed and clean shaven. I could smell the soap and shampoo lingering with the natural smell of his skin, and I felt the need for him rising. I quickly entered the steamy room and began my cleanup process. I was sticky with sweat and bodily fluids. My hair was a tangled mess, and I reeked of sex. By the time I was scrubbed clean and dressed, he was gone and so were the few things I was being allowed to take with me. There was a hazmat suit on top of the table, and I assumed they were watching and waiting for me to put it on. I grabbed a bottle of juice from the cooling unit and drank it all down. I was starving, and I did not know when I would get to eat so I ate some berries with granola and yogurt and a croissant before donning the bulky red suit.

It was only a matter of minutes before I heard the outer doors open. This time, they did not close and the people who entered did not remove their clothes. Four people entered, dressed in hazmat suits like mine, only theirs were yellow, not red. The inner door opened and they did not say a word, they just motioned with their hands that I should go with them. I did not recognize any of them, and they did not speak to me or even look at me on the walk through the labs. We emerged out of the laboratory and hospital wing and continued toward the town center. Everywhere I looked, things were different than they had always been. Everything that could be moved was gone, even the shrubs and trees.

If the shops and walkways had not looked the same, I would not have recognized this as my home. The streets and shops were empty. There was not a single person in sight, the usual sounds were also gone. No birds or music could be heard; there was only the sound of our boots against the cobblestone walkway and the sound of my breath in the helmet. Once we arrived at the center of the courtyard, I stopped and turned in circle, taking in my home for the last time. Where we were going most likely would be similar to this, but this was my world. The person in the yellow suit to my right nudges me forward a little aggressively, making me stumble a step or two. I guess this is the beginning of the gloves off stage of my captivity.

The hole the intruders created was not far off now, and we headed straight for it. One person dressed in yellow stood by the entrance. There was a single difference in his attire, as he held a very large gun across his chest. As we approached, he turned into the tunnel and took point. The four other others huddled around me as we walked deeper into the dark tunnel. About a hundred feet ahead of us, light is shining down from a gaping hole high above. At the bottom of the hole on the ground was a flat surface made of metal with cables attached at the corners. We made our way over and around the debris toward the makeshift elevator. The air around us was filled with dust and strange white particles. I had to remember to ask Graven or Z about it when I saw them. We positioned ourselves on the platform with me at the center, the man with the large gun in front of me facing away from me, and everyone else huddles so close to me that it was claustrophobic.

I looked up and the tunnel seemed to go on forever, and nothing but dust and haze could be seen. The walls of the tunnel were only a few inches larger than the platform, which was large enough to fit a vehicle on. There was a sudden jerk, and we were moving up at a steady rate. I wiggled a little to get them to give me some room, but it was to no avail. They remain glued to me, all facing away from me and all of them had weapons at the ready. The original four all had small handguns that were nothing like the giant weapon the man at the point was wielding. "Are you planning on being attacked? Should I be worried? Hello! Does anyone hear me?" I got no response from them at all. Maybe they can't hear me in this outfit and they have radio communication between them in theirs. Or they are just giant assholes. Could be either one. We were a long way down, and the platform moved slowly so the ride took over an hour.

I pictured Top Side being bright with light from the sun, but what I found was that there was little illumination in the thick cloud of particles surrounding us. I could not tell what was up or down and could barely see the point man. They nudged me forward and stuck to me like glue. Maybe they were afraid I would run and they would lose me in this storm or whatever it was. As I stepped off of the platform, my boots crunched something on the ground. The sound made me think of stepping on eggs or twigs, and it gave me a strange feeling in my gut that made me not want to look down. Not that I could see what I was stepping on through this muck, but I definitely did not want to know what it was. There was a line or rope of some kind attached to the platform base and the point man attached himself to it with a hook around his waist. Something large flew by my head and startled me knocking me off balance. Whatever it was, it left a smear across my faceplate and its appearance made our group move faster. We were running now, and I was barely touching the ground. They had me pinned and slightly lifted while they trotted. The point man was just slightly ahead of us with his gun raised, and he was sweeping back and forth. A shot rang out to my left side, and it was so loud I tried to cover my ears but my arms were pinned at my sides and I had that huge helmet on.

The man behind me bumped into me with a sudden jolt. He dropped his grip on my belt and began to jerk around frantically. Everyone stopped and turned toward him. I could barely see what was going on but it appeared that he had something attached to his thigh and they were desperately trying to get it off of him. The point man never turned around or helped; he just kept his gun pointed and swept back and forth. The man on the left did not help either and stood his ground with his weapon up. The other two were now crouched next to the man trying to pry off whatever had attacked him. It took several minutes for them to pull the blob off his leg and once it was loose, they dropped it on the ground and shot it. The man it had been attached to dropped to the ground and starts shaking like he is having a fit of some kind. His suit is torn and blood is running out of the hole. The other two look at each other and then turn back toward the man on the ground and shoot him through the helmet into his face. Then, like nothing had happened, they huddled around me and started the jog along the line again.

My head was spinning with all that I had just witnessed. How could they just murder their friend? Even if he was not a friend, he was at least a colleague. Doctors could have stopped the bleeding once we got to the caravan. Why leave his body like unwanted trash? While these thoughts swirled around in my head, I noticed lights not far in front of us. As we approached, I could make out large vehicles and yellow-clad guards pacing around. At the rear of the largest vehicle was a biohazard tunnel. My escorts, or at least what was left of them, pushed me into the tunnel and sealed the door. Immediately, a fine mist filled the air and then a forceful spray followed. The door at the other end opened and there stood Zaynep with a very worried look on her face. She motioned for me to remove my helmet and I did so. "Are you alright Enola?" she asked. I gave a little nod while I took off the rest of the suit.

She beckoned me toward the door, and I followed her into the dark space beyond. The door shut behind us and made a hissing sound as it sealed. Z wrapped her arms around me and hugged me tightly, all the while mumbling about being so worried and saying how it was so scary for them to move me during the day. I pushed out of her grip a little, "That was day time?" "Yes, and weird creatures come out in the day. That is why we only heard them digging down to us at night. We were running out of time to leave, so they decided to move you early in the day. I was so worried. No matter what precautions they seem to take, they always lose one or two people when they go out in the light."

I was given a quick tour of our new living space. We were in a Conex box on the back of a huge military truck. It was fourth feet long and seven feet wide. Toward the front was a makeshift bathroom with a toilet sink and hose attached to the wall with a wide nozzle for showering. This area had a three-foot wood wall and then just milky plastic from there up to the ceiling. There was not much privacy, but what did we really care about that? The water came from another Conex box on top of the one we were to live in. This tank held 800 gallons of freshwater that they had taken from New Eden. There was also another cabin on top of us that housed a few men and a sixty-caliber rifle stand for shooting apart obstacles such as debris from destroyed structures and rock that got in our way. We also had a small area for a kitchen with a mini-fridge and hot plate, a table, and five chairs. Rubbermaid containers held towels, supplies, and clothes. We were stocked up for two weeks, even though the trip to the main facility would only take three to five days, depending on obstacles along the way. There were no roads, street signs, or anything along the way to help us find our way back there. The rear area of the container had a large sleeping area set up like Z and I had our bedroom set up. There were lots of giant pillows and fluffy blankets.

"So, what happens next? And how will this thing get us all the way to your home?" Falcon took a deep breath, sat me down in a kitchen chair, and filled me in on the details of our journey. He began, "It would normally take us three days to travel that distance if we had no issues, encounters, or storms. The facility, Olympus, is somewhere around 788-800 miles from New Eden in North Eastern Montana. We are on a military semi-truck equipped with the best bulletproof siding and tires that are solid and cannot deflate. The problem is with its size and weight, it can only travel twenty to thirty miles per hour under ideal conditions. We won't have those. Additionally, there is the fact that we have to avoid areas that still have partial structures and intact underground facilities. Those are where we would most likely encounter the bugs.

Falcon went on, "Once we get to Eagle's Nest, the town that the Olympus facility took over, we will not have to worry about them. It used to be an American Indian reservation and museum located on and surrounded by thousands of acres of undeveloped land. Even the Bugs need to hide during the day, and they do not go around a lot of snow, so we will be safe." I could not wait any longer and interrupted, "Bugs? You mean to tell me that the only thing to survive the Blast were bugs and you are afraid of them?" "No, well I guess, yes. Okay, bugs did survive, some species, but the bugs I am referring to were once people. It was always a joke that bugs would be the only thing that survived the end of the world. So we call these humanoid creatures 'the Bugs' as a joke."

I had a moment of fear, "Are they what attacked us coming to the truck? Will they take over New Eden since you blasted a hole and breached us?" Falcon took my hand and gave it a small squeeze, "They are what attacked, but no they won't get in. We left people behind to tend to the facility. They will fortify New Eden and take care of the plants, animals, water makers, and electrical facilities. We will return there every six months to trade out people and get fresh supplies. That is how it works with all of the facilities we have located so far. Another thing we might as well get out of the way is that everyone knows you there by your actual name Eve. You are the first woman and they will all call you by that name. Your father insisted on calling you Enola, which is an acronym for some of the areas of scientific study that were involved in creating you, but your birth certificate and what everyone else agreed to name you was Evangaline. They raised you as their own and some of your DNA is from them, but there is also DNA from other top scientists, athletes, and more. The way the scientist sees it, you are theirs, all of theirs. Do you get me? I understand you have a lot of information to absorb and truths to suddenly believe. You do not understand how important you are to every human being who made it through to this point. Please, try to understand. You are the smartest person here so it should not take you but a minute to figure everything out once we get there."

I decided to chew on all I had learned about my role in this new world and ask questions about the Bugs. "So what do the Bugs look like, what do they do, and why do they try to kill people? Tell me about that. I am sure that is not classified information on a need-to-know basis." It was Graven's turn to tell me a tale. He became very animated while he spoke.

"Not everyone left in Top Side died quickly. Some must have had some kind of cover, not enough to survive like Falcon and hundreds of others, but just enough that they were still alive. They look almost melted like a candle, with their skin and fat bubbled over the exposed muscle. There are different levels of severity of burns radiation and mutilation. They are not zombies; you don't have to shoot them in the head to kill them, and if they get to you and you survive, you don't become one of them. They also do not sexually reproduce, so once we kill them all, it is over. The major problem is there are a lot more of them than there are of us. They have been burned down to the muscle and no longer have a working nervous system, so they do not feel pain when you fight them. They attack normal people to get our supplies, and they eat us since there are no other options available to them. Their brains are fried from radiation and heat exposure trauma, I assume. Some get together and have formed communities, but most just wander aimlessly attacking anything that moves."

He continued, " The ones that have grouped together are the most dangerous because they seem to have retained some cognitive abilities and work together like a pack of wild dogs. They put on clothes and equipment from the people they kill and stay out of sight during the extreme heat of the daytime. I have seen some who were covering their faces to keep the dust out of their mouth, nose, and eyes. One of the scientists had a theory that those Bugs could be brought back to normal human behavior, so we caught one and brought it to the lab. She manipulated the people dealing with her and ended up killing eight people before she was taken out herself. When they did the autopsy on her, small sections of her brain were still alive and the rest was like gooey tar. She still had her hypothalamus mostly intact, which is how she knew she was hungry and had to eat, and it was how she maintained blood pressure and body temperature. Parts of the cerebellum were still functioning, which is why she remembered basic skills but she had no potential for future learning. Her limbic system was a mess also. All this information led to the conclusion that the heat, radiation, trauma, and lack of sufficient nutrients and oxygen have left the Bugs with some basic skill memory, most autonomic bodily functions, and spurts of reasoning. They were aware of basic needs to survive but had no new information retention, no emotions, and these were not reversible. Some people actually argued to just avoid them and let them live out whatever the rest of their lives would be. While all this was being debated, a group of about fifty Bugs attacked a caravan out excavating an underground facility, killed everyone, and took the supplies. That ended the debate. We kill them all on sight, unless there are way too many for us to take on at once. We can't risk losing any human life, and we need them wiped out so that our future generations are not at risk from them. That is all I know, except that they are also squishy to the touch and smell incredibly bad."

Then, I asked, "But each one of them would have different damage to their brain just like the difference in severity to their outer skin right? Everything depends on what cover they had and any further damage since "the Day The Earth Shook." So, isn't it logical to reason that there is a great possibility that some of them have a lot less brain damage than she did?" Everyone looked at me and shrugged their shoulders. That was when Gnasta spoke up, "If we ever meet one that can talk, we may try to reason with it, but you will see. They are beyond all help. Some of the Bugs in the large groups seem to be able to reason as that woman did. We took her because she seemed the most intelligent. She appeared to listen when we spoke to her. Sometimes, she would smile and make familiar gestures. That is why her nurse ended up letting her guard down. But, Eve, she was just mimicking their actions, and my best friend was killed by her. She ate his face."

With that, Gnasta turned around and walked to the sink. She placed her hands on the counter and began to tremble. Graven walked up behind her and wrapped his arms around her. He is so much larger than she is that I could no longer see her from where I was sitting. I could still hear her crying and him whispering soothing words in her ear. I had never seen Gnasta act vulnerable in any way before and that made her pain seem so much worse somehow.

We all spend the next hour settling in and getting our new quarters organized and comfortable. When it came to the point that everyone was picking an area to sleep in and a place for their bedding, I saw Zeynep look at me and then another look exchange between her and Graven. "Don't get your panties in a wad Z, I already know about the three of you. I won't get jealous or in the way, I promise." All three seemed very surprised, " Um, we were just wondering if you would be sleeping with us, by yourself or..." she looked over at Falcon. " I think four would be a crowd. I'll make my area and we will see who ends up sleep where when the time comes."

There were glances all around, and I felt that things were going to be awkward at least for this first day. Gnasta and I have never been close to each other, and she still seems a little hostile toward me. Falcon made it clear that he was not going to be with me like that again. Graven, Z, and I were very comfortable together, which left out the other two. I missed Z and would prefer it be just us, but we would have to wait and see who got attracted to whom during the next few hours.

After setting everything up and chatting about the best places to put everything, we started to discuss what to have for dinner. We were all starving after having worked straight through past lunchtime. There was enough food for weeks but not much of a variety due to the confined space. "It is my fault we are all stuck in here, so I will try my best to put together something very special. Why don't the four of you go get cleaned up while I scrounge around for ingredients." Z walked over and put her arms around me. "I have a better idea. Why don't you come cleaned up with me and I'll wash your hair? I'll work my magic in the shower then you do yours in the kitchen. I've missed our alone time."

She gave me one of her mischievous smiles, took me by the hand, and started leading me to the shower area. We were giggling and almost skipping to the far end of the living quarters when Falcon spoke up, "Ladies, you know we should conserve water. Don't take too long, please." I gave him my sexiest smile, pulled my shirt over my head and threw it at him, exposing my large breasts and hitting him in the chest with the shirt. Z and I turned into the curtained-off area, took the rest of our clothes off, and tossed them out toward him. "Be a love and place those in the bin." The look on Falcon's face was priceless. He threw my shirt on the pile of the rest of the clothes at his feet. He walked over to us, grabbed me, and pulled me toward him.

"I thought I made it clear that fun time was over Eve. In a few days, you will have servants, and I am not one of them, never was, and never will be. Prancing around in front of me naked is not going to work either. Don't make this trip harder than it has to be. Have your fun with all of them, leave me be. You are all acting like we are on a field trip. The next few days are very dangerous for all of us. If we make it safely to Eagle's Nest, then you and Zaynep go to the tower and we go back to work. End of story. You will have plenty of time for sex games, in fact, that will be all you do once we get there." He did a rigid about face and walked away from us. Z and I looked at each other, "I guess he won't be joining us!" she whispered.

The Breath of God

Chapter Seventeen: The Transfer"

We turned on the water, which was warm due to the heat outside where the tank was. We washed each other's hair and only ran the water while rinsing. As I had my eyes closed and head led back to rinse my hair, Zeynep licked my nipple and continued up until she was gently nibbling on my chin then my lips. I tilted my head back down and slid my tongue into her waiting mouth. We only let it last a few moments as to not get Falcon back on his soapbox. "I've missed you so much, Enola. I am looking forward to eating one of your wonderful meals and then later eating wonderful you. I even brought our scarves so I can tie you up and tease you. Fuck the rest of them, I know where I am happy."

We kissed and caressed each other for a few more moments then we dried off and walked out to find some clothes. I had a towel around me but, as usual, Z was strutting her perfect body around like it was the most natural thing to do. She dug around in one of the bins and pulled out a matching pair of bright orange bra and panties. After slowly sliding the thong panties on, she turned her back toward Gnasta and asked her to hook her bra for her. Everyone was watching Z, we could not help it and she knew it. Gnasta obliged her and got a quick kiss for her effort. Zeynep then began searching the bin again and pulled out another matching bra and panty set, my favorite deep purple one, and it was not a thong, thank God. She tossed it to me and I walked back to the washroom area, finished drying off, and put them on.

My unruly curls were still a little damp when I walked back out to find her dressed in military pants and a t-shirt. Very un-Z-like. She had also laid out a matching outfit for me. "What is all this about? No miniskirts? No cleavage?" she smiled, tilted her head, and replied, "Apparently, we may have to, what did you call it Graven, Bug Out? " Graven grabbed my shirt from the chair it was dropped across and walked over to me, still standing there with damp curls and only my underwear on. "I usually prefer to take clothes off of you Beautiful, but if we run into trouble, we all have to be prepared to take off running. I can't bear to think of your perfect skin getting burned out there." I raised my arms, and he slid my shirt on. He moved his hands to each side of his face, looked deep into my eyes, and kissed me. It was ever so gentle at first but once I wrapped my arms around his neck and leaned my entire body into him, it became deeper and more urgent. I could see Gnasta leaning against the wall behind him. She rolled her eyes and crossed her arms. Obviously, she was going to be an issue like Falcon.

I pulled back, still sucking his lower lip as I did so. He let out a deep groan of pleasure but removed his hands from my face and turned to get my pants. "I am capable of dressing myself, you know." I took my pants from him and slipped them on. They were heavy material with lots of zippered pockets. They were not anywhere near as comfortable as my baggy overalls or sweats. I sat on the chair and put on the thick socks and boots. I had never worn stiff lace-up shoes like this before, but if they said I would need them to be safe, I would do it. As I fumbled with the laces, Falcon made a sound close to a giggle. He approached me, kneeled, and began to tuck the edge of my pants into the boots and lace them up. I could not help myself with him so close to me. I reached out my hand and began running my fingers through his hair. He did not pull away or say anything so I continued for a few moments. I let him finish the second boot without touching him. He looked up at me and I could tell by the look in his eyes that he wanted to say something, maybe wanted to kiss me, but he would not allow himself. I did not want to push things so soon into our journey so I just smiled and thanked him.

Zeynep and I started prepping for a dinner of cheese fondue with fresh veggies, fruits, and slices of bread for dipping. While we located the pans and ingredients, Graven and Gnasta took their turn in the shower. By the sounds coming out of there, it was obvious they were having a good time and enjoying each other to the fullest. It made me glad that I do not experience jealousy. Gnasta was trying to show me that she could have Graven whenever she wanted. Our kiss had made her territorial. The sounds of their lovemaking only made me want to join in, just like Falcon distancing himself from me only made me want him more.

Once the two lovebirds were done, Falcon took his turn alone. He was out and dressed very quickly and started setting the table for dinner. It was a very small table and we were crowded together around it, but fondue is meant to be a close dining experience. Each of them, even Gnasta, allowed me to feed them a few bites with their eyes closed and guessed what I had given them. Z and I used to do that every time we ate fondue. It is better with chocolate fondue and way more fun to lick off. We finished the meal, and Gnasta and Graven volunteered for cleanup duty. Z had brought my movie pad with her, so we began searching for a movie we thought the five of us could enjoy together. We decided on a comedy, "The Great Outdoors," with John Candy and Dan Akroyd. We all sat together on the beds as the movie played on the wall across from us. We had to push all the beds together to make it comfortable, so there went the whole sleeping separately idea.

Graven sat between Gnasta and Zaynep, then it was me, and, on the end, Falcon. It was not long before Graven and Z started caressing and kissing. Gnasta was not going to be left out and started to undo Graven's pants. She reached in and pulled out his erect penis and gave it a quick lick. Graven placed his hand on the back of her head and guided it further down until his penis was fully in her mouth and began a familiar rhythm. He had already pulled Zaynep's T-shirt and bra off and was sucking her nipple. My crotch was tingling and my nipples hard and aching. I attempted to cuddle closer to Falcon but he pushed away from me. "Please just kiss me," I moaned. He shook his head, not even looking at me. His eyes were glued to the wall where the movie was playing. "Feel free to join in. I have a job to do. Just leave me be, Eve." I sat back up straight, and Z pulled me down to kiss her. By this time, Gnasta had completed her task on Graven and was laying across his lap with her face buried in Zaynep's lap. Graven had his hand down the back of Gnasta's pants and was pleasuring her. As Z and I kissed, he went back to playing with her nipples with his other hand. I tugged my shirt over my head and tried to get my bra off. The tangle of bodies prevented me from reaching both hands behind my back.

"Falcon, please get this off for me, I can't reach it," I panted. I did not expect him to assist me but he did ever so gently undo my bra and slide it off of my shoulder. He also ran his hand down my spine. That sent tingles all over me. I slipped the rest of the way out of my bra as Z reached up and plucked at my throbbing nipples. She suddenly arched her back and let out a scream of pleasure. Graven wiggled out from the sitting position underneath her, crawled around to behind Gnasta, yanked her pants to her knees, and began fucking her from behind. She still had her face in Z, and she was still grinding into her and writhing around on the bed. When Zeynep was finished, she flipped onto her stomach and got me to face her. She tugged my pants off. Thankfully, I had removed my boots before climbing in the bed. I laid back and my shoulders and head landed in Falcon's lap. Graven and Gnasta had somehow fallen off of the bed and she now straddled him, riding him as they both made sounds of pleasure that made me ache and drip with anticipation.

Z began to lick me and run her fingers inside of me, which made me arch further into Falcon. I could feel his solid erection against the back of my head. I ran my hands up to my breasts and began to squeeze and rub them, all the while wiggling in Falcon's lap and grinding my crotch into Zaynep's face. I looked up at Falcon, and he had his eyes glues to the wall, pretending to watch the movie. He was determined not to participate, and it seems he was also going to pretend he was not aroused. That did not stop any of us. Graven and Gnasta were lying on the floor panting and smiling with after orgasm glow. I bucked and squirmed until I was also spent and sweating. Naked, I curled up against his side and stared up at him. He finally looked down at me and said, "You should clean up and get dressed. I told you we may have to leave quickly. You wouldn't last ten minutes out there naked." Then he turned his head back toward the movie. With a heavy sigh, I sat up gathered my clothes and sulked to the bathroom. When I came back out, the rest of them were dressed and watching the movie also.

Well, Gnasta was sitting next to Falcon, in my spot, watching it. Graven was sitting next to her with Z on his lap facing him. She was playing with his hair and every few minutes kissing his eyes, nose, or ears. I wanted to walk over and straddle Falcon the same way and just play with him like that, and I think he knew it was on my mind. Falcon looked over at me, whispered something to Gnasta, and stood up. Gnasta giggled like a teenager and almost skipped when she passed me on her way to the bathroom. Falcon followed behind her, undoing his belt and pants as he got near. He made sure once he was stepping behind the curtain to look back and see me watching. He grinned at me and winked! Oh my. The game is afoot. Gnasta would be doing whatever she could with my three lovers just to prove she could, and Falcon was going to let me get him all worked up but not touch me. He would let me see him get pleasure elsewhere. Playing games and being jealous makes no sense to me at all, I guess that is all part of my design to be a better human being, but a challenge intrigues me. I will have them both begging for me to touch them before we get to Eagle's Nest. I think I will work on Gnasta first so she will stop the needless competition for attention.

It was obvious that Falcon remained standing and Gnasta kneeled in front of him. I went to the kitchen and took out five glasses and a pitcher. I filled the pitcher with coconut water lemonade. I poured two glasses and brought them over to Z and Graven. We were all in need of replenishing fluids. They thanked me, and Z slid off of his lap to enjoy her beverage. As I got back to the table, Falcon emerged from the bathroom and I wordlessly handed him a glass. I grabbed a glass for Gnasta and walked to the bathroom entrance to catch her before she walked all of the way out. I held the cold glass to my chest, "I made you a cold drink. May I ask you a favor before you drink it? Your mouth has just been in my two favorite places. Can I kiss you and taste what you did, since I am the odd man out here?"

She tilted her chin up a little as she thought about it then stepped closer to me and took the glass. She set it on the counter and leaned toward me. I rubbed my thumb across her lower lip as I bit mine. I kissed her very gently, barely exposing my tongue. I sucked her lower lip into my mouth and tugged on it just a little. I made a groan and slid my hand around the back of her neck and pulled her face in closer. She pushed her tongue further inside my mouth and I responded the same. Still holding the back of her head with my right hand, I reached up with my left hand and lightly caressed her nipple with my thumb. It instantly became hard and we both moaned together.

I let go of her and leaned away from her just an inch and said, "Hmm, thank you Gnasta, that was sweet." I picked up her glass and handed it to her, turned, and walked away. I left the spot next to Falcon empty and sat between Graven's legs facing the movie. I leaned back on his chest. Zeynep was sitting next to him with her head on his shoulder. Graven had his right arm around Z, and he slid his left arm around my waist. He kissed the top of my head, and we snuggled together. There was an empty space between us and Falcon. Gnasta, still seeming a little dazed by our encounter, wandered over and looked at us for a moment before taking it. I could tell she was pondering the kiss. She had meant it to be a tease for me, but she had liked it and wanted more. She is stubborn and determined not to like me, much less to want me. I glanced over at her and smiled. She did not smile back, but I noticed her nipples were still solid as a rock. She was trying to decide to either cuddle up to Falcon or the pile of Graven, Zeynep, and I. She chose Falcon, and we all resumed watching the movie.

I woke up to Graven gently trying to squirm out from under me. Falcon and Z were fast asleep. Gnasta was tossing and trying to get comfortable. Graven slid down on the bed from the seated position he had been in. We were still wrapped up in each other as he did. His movement ended with us face to face, and we immediately devoured each other's lips. I could feel his chiseled muscles beneath his shirt and rubbed my body against his even harder. Gnasta was behind me and Zeynep was behind him. I could tell Z was still asleep. I've spent years watching her sleep. I could see the familiar breathing pattern the softness of her facial features.

I sighed thinking about how much I loved her. Graven thought I was reacting to his attempts to take off my shirt. I lifted my arm and made it easier for him. He dipped his head toward my breasts, and I arched back a little to put place my nipples in a better position. As I moved, I felt Gnasta move behind me. She was facing us now. I could feel her eyes on me. Graven pulled me toward and under him. He skillfully removed my pants and his shirt. He kissed me while squeezing my face in his hands. His hands and lips moved lower with each kiss. As he began tongue teasing me, I could not help but thrust into him, moan, and wiggle. He finished me quickly and kissed his way back to my face. I loved the taste of my pleasure in his mouth.

I reached down and undid the buttons of his fly. He helped me push his pants down, and I used my feet to get them off the rest of the way. I took his hands and placed them on the wall above my head and pushed him toward the wall above me. He immediately understood what I wanted and slid his body over me until he was hovering above my face. I gripped his balls with my left hand and firmly tugged on them. He tilted his head back and groaned with pleasure. With my right hand, I pulled his throbbing erection down and slid it into my mouth. Graven began to rhythmically pump into me, faster and harder while I flicked my tongue in circles around the head and shaft.

I could tell he was about to release so I slid my finger into his anus and mimicked his rhythm on my face. He screamed my name as he came, waking Falcon, who gave him an angry look before laying back down with his back toward us. Graven rolled off of me and was sitting with his back against the wall between Z and me. He was sweating and panting with his hand on my breast. I looked over at Gnasta, who was on her side facing me. "Do you want a taste from me now? I would love to return the favor." She did not immediately decline so I turned toward her and kissed her. I pulled her hand up to my naked sweaty breast and moaned in her mouth as she rubbed my nipple. I knew that during and right after sex my pheromones were especially crazy and overpowering.

Graven was then lying down behind me and began rubbing my back and ass. Falcon rolled over toward us, with Gnasta between us, and gave me an angry glare. I whispered to Gnasta, "Can I take off your shirt?" and she reached to untuck it, but it was Falcon who pulled it off of her. I lowered my face to her breasts and started gently nuzzling and kissing. Falcon reached around and began fondling her left breast while I was sucking the other. I tilted my head up, and she found my lips with hers. Falcon abandoned her nipple and had his hand down her pants. She began to pant and arch into him. Damn, he was stealing her from me. He rolled her over on top of him now facing away. Together, they struggled to get her pants off. Falcon was already naked. He must have taken his clothes off while she and I were making out. She sat up and leaned a little forward, allowing him access to thrust his engorged penis into her. She rocked back and forth with his hands on her hips and her hands on his thighs. I ran my hands down his rippled chest and abs. I wanted him inside me like that. I reached my hand to his face and turned it toward me. His expression softened and he returned my stare.

I attempted to kiss him, but he turned his face away. He gripped her ass and pushed her up and down faster. She cried out a few seconds before he pushed her off, and then he finished himself off. He knew exactly what he was doing to me. I had just watched him enter her, which he could never do to me, then I watched him cum and I knew it was not because of me. He was very much determined to show me he did not need or want me. Graven saw this also. He knew I was worked up and wanted Falcon. He pulled me back against his naked body and pushed my thighs apart enough to get his fingers in just the right place. He began kissing my neck and back while twirling his fingers. Again, Gnasta was watching. She moved closer and kissed me, slowly and gently at first but then with hunger and need. She slid her hand down and met Graven's. They both fondled me and kissed me until I was bucking and shaking. The release was sweet as always, but I still longed for Falcon and to have real sex the way we are built to have it.

Chapter Eighteen: A Rough Ride

We woke with a jolt as the huge tires climbed over debris. It had been a bumpy ride the entire time, but now it felt as if we were driving over large rocks or mounds of some kind. There was no way for us to tell if it was night or day outside. The container had no windows and no way for the light to penetrate inside. There was an intercom box on the wall near the bathroom. Graven made it to the box, stumbling with each large jolt, and pressed the button. "Everything okay up there? We are getting a hell of a ride back here." He took his finger off of the button and stumbled, almost falling this time as the container rocked from side to side violently.

The speaker in the box squealed and a voice I presume came from the front cab said we were having to go a different path than the one they took getting to our facility. The other path had too many Bugs and visibility was compromised from the wind. I glanced around at Falcon and Gnasta to see if they were nervous or apprehensive in any way. Zeynep and I were new to this, but they had been down this road before, so to speak. They were both putting on their boots, but they did not look overly concerned with the news. "I'd get your boots on ladies. Better to be prepared for the worst than risk getting caught with your pants down."

With that said, Falcon stood up and cautiously made his way to the kitchen. Graven was already in the bathroom, and Gnasta was crawling in that direction. I scooted over to Z and hugged her. She looked worried and I hated to see that look on her beautiful face. I had not brushed my teeth yet so I did not kiss her, though I wanted to. She placed her head on my shoulder for a few minutes then we put our boots on as well.

By the time we staggered to the kitchen like drunken sailors on a ship being tossed around at sea, the other three were done using the bathroom. Zeynep used the toilet while I brushed my teeth then we switched positions. We stumbled our way to the table, and I sat down as she began brushing out my tangled red mass of curls. Gnasta was watching us as Falcon attempted to make coffee. She jolted over to us and stood with Z behind me. "Let's braid it. That will keep it out of the way and tame it down. We could enter twine them Viking style, that would look great with color."

Zeynep replied," I have never had long hair, I don't know how to braid. I am sure I would catch on if you start it." For the next hour they were at it, braiding, talking, giggling, and kissing that I heard occasionally.

I drank the coffee that Graven brought to me, even though I do prefer tea. It was better than just sitting there like a lump. I used to Z messing with my hair and putting makeup on me like I was her life-size doll. "My sister, Robyn, has long hair. It is red also, just not this crazy color. We use to spend hours doing each other's hair when we were little. I cut mine after all this happened. She still keeps hers long. In my line of work, it is not practical. Just something else a Bug could grab on to or for radiation dust to cling to." I asked her, "So your sister is at Eagle's Nest?" "Yes, you will meet her. She works in the tower, so you will be spending time with her every day once we get there. I'm sure she will love doing your hair. You see, she will be yours. She will lay out your clothes, run your bath, do your hair, prepare you food, whatever you require of her. She will also report back to Caesar on how you are doing, what you are doing, and what you need. She is already living in the tower with the others," Gnasta informed me. "Other girls like me?" I was hoping that was the case. "No Enola, there is no one else like you. Not even the men are exactly like you. You are the first, very unique, and even unclonable. Enola spelled in a mirror is Alone. You alone will resurrect mankind."

Zeynep ended the conversation by saying, "Tada!! Look boys, what do you think? We are finally done, but I believe it was worth it." Falcon gave a half-smile but did not comment. Graven walked cautiously over to stand in front of me. He ran his fingers through the one long curl they left free hanging down my jawline past my breast. "You look good enough to eat," he purred at me. "Ladies, you outdid yourselves. I think you each deserve a kiss. Don't you?" That statement prompted more giggling from all three of us.

We ate our breakfast while still being jolted around with little conversation. Each of us was concentrating on keeping our food and drink from flying off the table. There was nothing we could do about the bumpy ride, and we had nothing to do inside the container but read, watch movies, and interact with each other. None of those options seemed to be easy under these conditions. We chose to turn on some background music and just lie around doing nothing.

Our absolute boredom and carnival ride lasted for three days. Once the ride became smooth again, we were all exhausted. We had not been able to get much sleep during the Tilt A Whirl experience so we all flopped on the pillows and slept soundly. I woke up to the smell of someone cooking something Italian. The aroma of basil, oregano, thyme, and tomatoes filled the container we called home for the last six days. It felt good to not wake up alone and for someone else to be cooking. My time in the containment chamber was all but a memory now. Everyone seemed to be in a much better mood as we all stretched and got up out of bed. Gnasta was the one in the kitchen cooking, and she had soft music playing as she swayed to the music while stirring her stir fry. We all freshened up and sat down to a delicious meal that did not try to escape our plates. We chatted about the past few days and how annoying it was. Everything seemed back to normal for the most part.

Chapter Nineteen: Soon to Arrive

Falcon pressed the intercom button and inquired about our progress. The voice through the box informed us that we should arrive first thing in the morning. Thank Goodness! We will finally get out of this box. That was my reaction, but not so much that of the others. The rest of my travel companions seemed to get a bit melancholy at his mention of us arriving at our destination soon.

Gnasta said, "I guess we should get everything tidied up and packed away before we go to sleep. That way, once we arrive, all we have to do is grab our stuff and go." "Sounds like plan to me. We should get up early and do Enola's hair again. I want her to walk in to the own looking like a conquering and beautiful shield maiden. Everyone will be there to try to get a glimpse of her anyway, so let's give them a show," Z said. "Wait a minute, why is my arrival going to be like a circus? Doesn't that seem like, well, crazy?" I asked

Falcon chimed in, "We have been searching for you for five years. Ever since we came together as a community our entire goal has been to set up a new city and find you. We sent teams to every facility we have been able to find, and ours found you. It will be a very big deal. We always come back with livestock, vegetation, medications, people, and supplies. Yes ,we also bring one hybrid if they are still there, but none of them are you. There is only one Eve, and maybe we have not told you the entire story, and we should before we arrive. Not only are the others not as perfect as you, not as detailed and advanced as you, but they are all male." They all just stared at me waiting for my response. "Well, that makes sense, I'm supposed to be the mother of the new world, right? I guess my suitors are very diverse, representing different cultures and nationalities. That is how I would have set it up. How many of them are there and am I expected to get pregnant by each one?" "There were eight when we left to find you. Could be more now if the two other teams are back," Graven stated.

Gnasta became a little bit more excited at his point. "I have met them. Would you like me to tell you about your harem?" I nodded, sat down and listened, taking it all in as best I could. "First we found Djorg. He is mahogany black, completely hairless with strong African features, and very athletic. He is a biologist and master of anatomy and physiology. He has black eyes with no whites at all. He is very friendly, actually kind of playful. Our next find was Olaff; he is tall, strong, broad-shouldered, blonde haired, and has crystal clear eyes. He's very militant. And an expert in games and theory, strategy, logistics, hand to hand combat, and physics. He is a tad rigid, quiet but bossy. Number three is Phang Lee. He has a small build and dark short hair, an Asian appearance, orange eyes with vertical slits, and he's an expert at martial arts, dance, art, and philosophy. He is even more intense than Olaff.

The next one they found was found by my team. I may be a little biased but he is my favorite. Caspian has olive skin and the most stunning bright green eyes and shoulder length brown hair. He is an excellent chef, linguist, an expert in sociology, history, and religions. He's the epitome of a sexy, romantic gentlemen. Then we have the kind of strange one named Raven Wing. He possesses long black hair to his waist, which he is always worn in a single braid down his back. He has medium brown skin, yellow eyes with no pupil at all, and is very trim and muscular. I have never seen him wear a shirt. He is always wearing pants and leather laceup boots and nothing else. He's an expert in tracking, hunting, plants, herbs, and is the keeper of the ancient ways. He's very serious- no nonsense- I never have spoken to him or seen him smile."

She went on, "Valcor is a blast. He has blonde surfer hair, lightly tan skin, and an athletic body. He is a marine biologist and veterinarian. He's suave, laid back, and always telling jokes. Next, we have Haymich, with red curly hair and white pale skin just like yours. But he has dark blue eyes with no whites. It is hard to look at his eyes but who needs to? He is broad-shouldered and very tall. His expertise is highlander studies, geology, and mathematics. He has a loud, contagious laugh. Last, but not least in any way, is the extremely gorgeous Sterling. He has silver, not gray, metallic-looking hair that is perfectly straight and long. His eyes are bright white with black vertical slits. He is very pale like you with a medium build and carries himself very gracefully. He's a genetic biologist, chemist, and all-around scientific genius. He has a gorgeous smile, but he seemed very shy when I met him. So basically they covered African, Italian, Norwegian, American Indian, Asian, a total Surfer dude, Scottish, and something like Icelandic. Well, so far. Who knows what they found while we have been gone. That is just in this continent. We have no idea what if anything is going on around the world."

I sat listening to her, my head spinning with the information I was given. I looked over at Zaynep, and she sat very still just watching me. Falcon was keeping busy tidying up the kitchen with his back toward me and apparently there was something very interesting on the bottom of Graven's shoe. I could tell there was more to the story but Gnasta was just going to tell me all about my chosen lovers to keep things on the light side. While she still rambled on about the men I would be living with, I thought about all the questions I had. I could only have one or two babies every nine months unless they had a way to make me have quintuplets each time. That is still a handful of babies a year and they could not produce their own children for at least sixteen years.

This seems like a very slow process for them to be going to all this trouble over me. What about cloning? What advances have they made in the genetic alteration process they used to create me? Why was theref only one of me? I knew better than to voice my apprehensions since each time in the past they all refused to come clean. Gnasta sighed, "You aren't even listening to me, are you?" "I am sorry, I guess my mind wandered off there for a few moments. Wow. Sounds like I'm going to have my hands full." I got up from my chair and walked over to Falcon, who still had his back to me. I wrapped my arms around his slim waste and buried my head between his shoulder blades. He did not try to pull away from me. Graven came up behind me and sandwiched me between them. He wrapped his arms around Falcon's chest and rested his chin on the top of my head. We stayed like that for a few minutes before Falcon pushed back a little, turning in my grip to face me. He placed his strong hands on each side of my face and tilted it up toward his. Our eyes met, his were filled with tears, and it moved me deep in my chest. "It will all be okay. They will love you even more than we do. I guarantee it." He ran his thumb over my lips then gently kissed me.

Chapter Twenty: Waking Up

It was morning and the collective mood in our little hovel was somber. Last night we cooked, ate, and cleaned up. We packed everything in the kitchen away that we did not need for a quick meal this morning. No movies that night, it was just quiet music and books. Falcon slept next to me and held me in his arms all night. The sexual frolicking of the previous nights was gone but not forgotten. We should have spent all evening enjoying each other since after today, I would never see any of them again except for Zaynep, but they all seemed sad and stayed to themselves. I knew I should feel sad, but that is something I guess they programmed out of me. I knew I would miss them, especially Falcon, but I had hopes of seeing him again.

Gnasta and Z spent a lot of time on my hair and they picked out my clothes. I had to wear think clothing and boots to get from the caravan to the facility entrance, but then they wanted me to change into a one shoulder flowing gown of emerald green. It made me picture Athens and the Greek togas, but the color did accentuate my red hair and purple eyes. I did not know what to expect, confetti, a band, or maybe speeches? Did the people want me there and all agree with their ideas of repopulating through me? How many thought like Gnasta that I am an abomination and not a human at all? It all remained to be seen.

Once we were all dressed and our backpacks secure, they began tying us to one another's waists. There was a metal clasp for a quick disconnect just in case. I very glad they think ahead, but it sure did not inspire confidence. I was given a long, drawn out speech about moving quickly, don't stop to help anyone, and if the worst happens, just run like hell and they will find me. Not a very complicated plan at all.

It was time to say our goodbyes. Apparently, once we got inside the facility, we would be separated and my hand maiden, Robyn, would be the one to dress me. The boys and Gnasta would be off to the head of the procession while Zaynep and I would follow, surrounded by guards. It all sounded like a crazy parade, and I was anxious to get it over with. It was time to put the hazmat suits on and prepare to leave.

The truck came to a sudden stop and not a split second later, the back door swung open. I could not see a thing outside except for debris violently blowing in the air. A man appeared on each side of the door in dark think military-looking gear and clamped on to each side of Falcon's waist belt. Falcon stepped down quickly and just as fast, two more men appeared and hooked on to Gnasta. I was next in line, then Zaynep. Graven pulled up the rear and as soon as he was out, the doors slammed shut and the truck began to move away from us. The wind gusts were at least 75 miles per hour and full of black blobs that made a squishy sound as they hit our gear. So, there we were, tied together in a line with two men on each side of us, jogging toward more darkness. It had to be nighttime, according to what I have been told about the outside world. During the day, it is supposed to be over 180 degrees and bright. You can't see the sky or sun, but the rays of the sun illuminate the thick air and allow for a little bit of visibility.

We were only jogging for maybe three minutes before we came to a halt. I still could not see a thing past the person in front of me, but I heard a loud cranking noise very close to us. After a minute or two, we began walking forward and as soon as I thought we were going to start jogging again, the loud cranking noise started again behind us. Once the noise stopped, lights came on all around us. There were people in hazmat suits surrounding us and looking all around the small room we were in. I guessed they were making sure that no Bugs followed us in. Just as suddenly as the lights had come on, a mist started to fill the room. It reminded me of the steam room at the gym. Everyone just stood still, and no one spoke a word. Once the steam cleared, a door opened, and we all filed through to another much larger room with seats and lockers along the walls.

One of the armed guards walked up to Falcon and gave him one of those manly half hugs with back slapping. They seemed to be talking, but I could not hear anything with the helmet on. Another guard began unhooking us from one another while the others began taking off their hazmat suits and hanging them up. Someone from behind me removed my helmet for me. I did not realize haw heavy and uncomfortable it was until it was off. I rolled my neck and shoulders around to work out the kinks and realized they were all staring at me. Oh boy, this is uncomfortable, and there are only six of them. What is it going to be like when I enter the city? I raised my hand wiggled my finger and said, "Hi." I got nothing back. Five men and one woman just continued to stare at me.

I turned toward Zaynep, who was completely out of her suit now and helping to undo mine. "Do I have a buggar?" I asked. She giggled, "They aren't supposed to talk to you. Only Caesar and those who live in the tower are allowed to be anywhere near you or speak to you. I know it all sounds strange but you are like royalty to some and a demon to others. Don't even think about it, we will be in the tower soon. I am sure they will parade you through town first to display their prize and all that. They want to show everyone that you do exist and all the promises that have been made will be kept. Now, let's get you into that awesome dress."

Everyone left the room except for Falcon and Z. Though another door, a girl came in carrying flowers. She was as short as me with long, straight red hair and a cherub face. Her smile was infectious. She practically danced over to me. This had to be Robyn, Gnasta's little sister. She actually bowed in front of me and presented the flowers to me. I took them and thanked her. She seemed to be vibrating with energy and started talking very rapidly. "I am so excited to meet you. I'm Robyn, your servant, and I don't take my position lightly. This is such an honor. I can't believe you are really here and how perfect you are and that you spoke to me, too." Everyone except Robyn began laughing when she took a breath. It was just what we needed to relax a little. The tension in the room before Robyn entered could be cut with a knife. Her joviality and enthusiasm were infectious. She was not like Gnasta at all. All dressed up like a Greek Goddess, I walked to the door to meet the people of the city.

Chapter Twenty-One: Eagle's Mess

The doors were opened by two armed guards. There was a path for me to walk down followed by my escorts that was about five feet wide and lined with more armed guards. We were elevated a little as we exited the entrance room, and I could see a large part of the city. At New Eden, our Town Center had tress, bushes and flowers, and pebble walkways with koi ponds and gazebos. This was not New Eden at all. Everything was dirty and gray. Every inch was covered in small tents and thrown together shacks. It reminded me of the towns in the "Mad Max" movies. People wore ragged clothes and were washing them in buckets next to the tents. There were no roaming animals, no birds, and no one under the age of twenty. As looked closer there were also no older people; the oldest person I saw was a man who appeared to be in his fifties.

There were also no parade noises, no shouts or cheers or confetti waiting for me. Half the people were not even paying attention to what was going on, like a pure blood entered every day dressed like a Goddess and had an armed walkway. Others were lined up behind the guards staring at me some with awe and some with malice. I am not sure what I expected, but it was not this. Falcon gave me a nudge and I started to walk forward with him at my side. Robyn came up on my left side and took my hand; she was almost skipping. "She's here, she's here!" she shouted as she held my hand up and did a spin underneath it as if we were dancing. Her enthusiasm did cause some of the people to start acting excited and laugh and cheer, but the others looked at me like I was there to kill them all. I held my head high and refused to look scared or upset at their leers."

I saw the Tower off in the distance and it was lit up with people looking out of the windows. I quickened my pace to match that of Robyn's and kept my eyes on it. The walk was over a mile, and as we got closer to the Tower, the facility became less crowded and cleaner. Two blocks away, the tents and shacks stopped and lawns with trees and flowers that surrounded the Tower began. I took a deep breath and looked at my escorts, "Well, that was not uncomfortable at all, was it?" Falcon took me by the arm and ushered me forward to the bridge that led to the Tower doors. He said, "The penthouses are on the top floors, and yours is the highest. Below you live the rich members of the facility, the Mayor and council.

Falcon continued, "Below that is where the scientists and engineers live. The rest of the building is laboratories. That is all you need to be concerned with. Once you go in the Tower, you will not be coming out here. If you need anything, Robyn will get it. Caesar will meet us at the door with the council members, and after a meeting and banquet, they will escort you to your floor. Robyn and Zaynep will accompany you from here; this is as far as we are permitted." He brushed his thumb over my lips then kissed me very gently while holding my face in his hands. There were tears in his eyes, I swear it. "I'll never forget you, my love," he whispered to me and then abruptly turned and walked away with all the guards.

Robyn and Zaynep each grabbed one of my hands and started walking me over the bridge. Robyn stopped to pick a big, beautiful, purple flower from a bush and slipped in in my hair. "That will bring out your crazy purple eyes!" she giggled. The bridge spanned a small pond filled with lily pads and brightly colored fish. There were ducks and swans lazily floating around the picturesque scene. All I could think of was the contrast from this setting to that of a few blocks away. Was it because of overcrowding? I had a lot of questions that I knew would not be answered today. I had to go to a meet and greet first and then dinner. My curiosity would have to be put on hold until tomorrow.

The ornate mahogany double doors to the Tower opened, revealing twelve people standing there waiting for us. All of them were dressed as I was, with bold colored flowing gowns and robes. The women had their hair woven with gold bands, flowers, and scarves high on their heads. They were all smiling and whispering to one another. They were the council, with the mayor at the head on the left and Caesar on the right, two steps ahead of the group. I looked at Zaynep, and she mouthed the word, "Wow," to me, then put on her best smile and pushed forward.

Chapter Twenty-Two: Meet the Family

We arrived at the steps to the Tower door, and as we did, the Caesar began descending the steps to meet us. He held out his hand to me, and I let him envelop my hand in his. "What a glorious day my dear, you are finally here. I trust you had a pleasant trip. Come let me introduce you to the city council." Not waiting for an answer, he grabbed me away from the girls by my upper arm and walked me up the remaining steps. I was introduced to each person in turn. Each one kissed me very tenderly on the lips and when that was done, they turned and walked away into another room down the hall. It was all done quickly, and I never had a chance to even look around before I myself was whisked away to the same room down the hall. What I did see were highly polished marble floors, tapestries on the walls, and antique furniture. It was so very different than the living conditions outside.

The room we entered was even more impressive and large. On each side of the room were long tables with silk table clothes, candles, flowers, and a plethora of gourmet foods and wines. Large bowls of fruit, trays of cheeses, baked breads, whole chickens, ducks, and a pig. There was no way we could eat even half of the food laid out for us. Would they give the rest to the people outside? At the end of the room were two tables set up for dining. One had all of the chars on one side facing the room and other table. The other table had twelve settings of fine china, silver utensils, and crystal water and wine glasses. The head table had large very plush ornate chair in the middle with five seats on either side all set with the same fine dining paraphernalia as the other table.

The council members all walked to their assigned seats and stood behind the chair. Caesar walked me to the ornate chair in the middle of the other table and even helped me sit in it like a gentleman. Zaynep sat on my right and Robyn on my left. Once we were seated, the council members sat, too. Caesar sat with them with the mayor at his side. I did not notice until then that there was a small group of musicians sitting in a dark corner playing soft music. I could make out a harp, cello, and violin. The scene was extravagant and over-the-top gaudy.

One of the servants walked to the door and opened it. He then spoke in a loud voice to be heard by all over the chamber music. "May I present to

Eve, Djorg." A tall vary dark man entered dressed more like a knight than like the council's Greek-themed garments. He wore tight pants with tall leather boots and a button down ornate sleeveless shirt with a leather belt. He briskly walked to the table and bowed at me. He never broke eye contact, smiled, and said, "I pledge my love, loyalty, and protection to my Eve." He walked around the table, took my hand in his, and kissed it. He placed a bracelet on my wrist that looked like ivory. He took the seat next to Z and never even acknowledged either of my escorts. The same ritual was performed by each of the men as they entered. Each was announced as they entered, and each pledged himself to me. The only difference was in how they greeted me upon walking around the table.

Olaff kept his distance, handed Robyn a tiny puppy with a bow, gave me a little smile then sat. Phang Lee presented me with a lotus flower armband made of jade and kissed me on the forehead before sitting. Caspian got down on one knee, placed an emerald ring on my finger, and gently kissed my lips. Raven Wing gave me a dream catcher with a single black feather hanging from it. Valcor gave me an anklet made of seashells and took my face in his hands and rubbed noses with me. We both giggled at that as he sat. Haymich picked me up in a bear hug and twirled me around. He said, "May I kiss you, Lass?" and with my nod, kiss me he did. I swear it lasted five minutes, and his tongue tickled my toes from the inside. He gave me a beautiful necklace shaped like a vine. Sterling was last, but for sure, not least. He was amazingly gorgeous and his mere presence made me tingle in special places. He kissed both my eyes and placed a thin platinum crown on my head. With all the introductions made and gifts given, the Caesar proclaimed it time to eat.

The council wandered around the banquet table, filling their plates and talking with each other. No one moved from my table. I was not sure if we were supposed to mingle or not. They forgot to give me instruction pamphlets on the proper etiquette for this occasion. I looked to Robyn for guidance, and she smiled and informed me that I needed to go first or send her for a plate. I looked down the line each way at the people at my table and asked, "Am I the only one who thinks all this weird? " I could tell by the looks on their faces I was not alone. Djorg whispered, "It is best to just go with the flow. Caesar has his moods, always stay on his good side. If they want to play dress up and party, then go along. It does not happen often. You will see." I smiled at him and nod. We all got up together and merged in with the others.

I filled a plate with a little of everything and returned to my seat. My water glass had been filled while I was away, and I noticed that no one at our table had wine glasses. The council members were all drinking wine and had already seemed to have forgotten that we were even there. "So, we don't get wine. I've never had any before so I really don't care, but is that the way it is? None for us?"

Haymich's booming voice answered me, "We were all raised like you- the only of our kind in a facility with a companion to keep us company. We have never been outside, never had liquor or anything unhealthy whatsoever. The only difference is that we were told what we are and what we were created for. I heard about you my whole life. I am not disappointed so far." He laughed and blew me a kiss. When everyone was full, the council members said their goodbyes and left the banquet hall. Caesar dismissed my harem and my escorts also. He and I waited until everyone was gone before we stood and walked to the door. "I'm sure you have a lot of questions. We will talk soon." With that said, he waked me to an elevator that was waiting with the door open. We chatted about the meal on the ride to the top floor. The door opened and he motioned for me to exit, as soon as I did, the door closed behind me and he was gone.

Robyn was waiting for me down the hall and led me to my rooms. Yes, plural rooms. There was a dressing room filled with clothes, shoes, and jewelry. There was also a bathroom with a tub big enough for five people to bathe in comfortably, a bedroom with the largest bed I could ever imagine with lots of pillows, very ornate dressers, an armoire, and several lounging couches. Everything was dark wood, gold tasseled and bold other colors of green, purple, and burgundy. The next room had a stone fireplace, shelves of books, and pillows the size of couches all over the floor. My new puppy was asleep in a bed next to the fireplace. It was a pure white fluffy little thing. Where was it supposed to use the bathroom locked up on the twentieth floor? I know, strange that this is what I am worrying about at this point in the evening.

Down the hall was a kitchen and a dining room with a table large enough for us all. Further down the hall were eight more bedrooms (one for each of the men), several other sitting rooms, and a few vacant ones. Robyn explained that she and Zaynep live in my quarters while the men have a private room each. She and Robyn were not allowed in their rooms, ever. I, of course, was expected to make myself at home anywhere on this floor. The companions of the men had quarters on the third floor down and they were sent for if they were needed or wanted for anything. Robyn was allowed to leave this floor, but the rest of us were not authorized to enter the elevator unless escorted by Caesar.

We returned to the main room with the fireplace, and all the guys were in there waiting. They had all changed clothes to more casual attire and looked a lot more at ease. I walked over to the puppy and picked her up, snuggling her to my chest. "Does she have a name?" I asked the room of men with their eyes all on me. Ollaff his voice very low and timid, "I was waiting for you to officially name her. I've been calling her Puff for the few days she has been here." "Does she like it?" I asked. " No, not really, she just ignores me." "I'm just having trouble picturing you with a dog named Puff. You are so very big and intimidating. Did you pick her out for us?" I asked and he smiled big. "Yes I did, thinking that a delicate woman would want something she could carry around in a purse. If I had met you first, I would have gone with my first choice." " And what was that?" I asked him. " A Doberman or Shepperd. They are fine, protective dogs."

" I would have loved anything you chose for me, Ollaff. It was very sweet of you. I love all the gifts I was given tonight. I was not expecting this or I would have gotten something for each of you. Of course, I did not even know about any of you until the trip here, so that would have made my options for gifts limited to granola bars." Everyone had a little giggle while I put Puff down. Robyn picked her up and announced that she was going to take her potty. Everyone began to sit down on the floor cushions, except me. I needed to get out of this dress and get comfortable also.

Chapter Twenty-Three: Oh My!

I asked the room of men, "Could one of you help me get this belt off? I'm not sure how to get it undone. I need to get comfortable like you did. " Caspian was closest to me and was on his feet and behind me quicker than I could blink. He smelled of jasmine and cedar and his hands were soft and swift at his task. He gently kissed the back of my neck as he removed my belt. My mouth went dry and my knees quivered a little. Om my, I know I have a high libido, but how could I possibly handle eight men? What did they expect of me? Nothing had been explained to me about any of this.

I turned toward him, " I am a little nervous, I don't know what you all expect of me. I was not informed of anything about any of this until the men broke into our facility. Don't get me wrong, I am not shy, I just would like to get to know everyone. Okay?" He kissed my lips using his tongue to gently part them a little. I responded in kind. "None of us will push you Eve. We realize how overwhelmed you must be. We are one big happy family now. You know we don't get possessive or jealous. We have all been here a while, some of us even for years. Sterling was born here in this facility. We don't think Caesar will push you to get pregnant tonight," he teased.

"Well, is there a plan of some type? Do I get pregnant by each of you? That will take years." "Lass, Ceasar will go over details later. We know that he wants you to pick one, get pregnant, and while you are pregnant, you can sleep with whoever else you want. Then it goes to whoever is next in line to get you pregnant. You decide the order or we can draw straws. That is all up to you. Each of us has to get you pregnant, but when that is done, it is all your choice who you like or don't. We could always call for our companion, but you are the only woman we can have real relations with. You also have Zaynep and Robyn to please you if you get tired of men." Again came his booming laughter. Even with the strange information he just given me, I had to laugh with him.

"Well, I guess you guys will need to draw straws, as there is no way I could possibly choose on my own. I'll go get changed and find Z, but before you guys get too excited, I am not perfect. I talk too much, get annoying, eat all the time, and am naughty." With that, I dropped my dress off of my shoulders and stepped over it, walking to my dressing room. Valcor exclaimed, "Now that is what I am talking about!"

I entered my dressing room and found Zaynep sitting in a chair waiting for me. "What happened to your dress? I could swear you had clothes on last time I saw you." I explained to her how I felt like a horse on display for potential buyers, so I showed them teeth. We both got a good laugh and picked out a pair of cream-colored linen pants and a spaghetti strap green linen shirt. I slipped into a pair of sandals, and we returned to the main room. Robyn had returned from walking Puff, and she had my dress in her hands. "Oh, thank you. I was just coming to retrieve that." "No problem ma'am, I will go hang it up for you. Is there anything you need?" I stopped mid-stride and looked at her.

I told her, "You are not a slave, and my name is Enola. Please call me Enola. I'm not Eve, I'm not special, and I'm not anything more than anyone else. If we are all to live together as one big happy family, then get it through your heads to treat me like you treat each other. Relax and be yourselves. Which reminds me of a question. Since you cannot have sex with these guys, who are you and Z supposed to, you know, be friendly with?" "Well"]," she blushed, "They all have companions downstairs, men and women. We can be with them or if you invite us to join in with you we can, but we just can't do anything except for play. Do you know what I mean?"

Chapter Twenty-Four: On a Silver Platter

Zaynep and I watched Haymich light the fire while the other men moved the cushions closer together in front of it. The men had gone ahead and drawn straws for their pregnancy placement. To my grand delight, Sterling won first placement, so he was who I shared a cushion with now. We all spent the evening talking about the banquet and the ridiculous amount of food that was prepared. They all laughed when I said I was hungry again and all agreed that we needed a snack. Robyn called down and asked to have some leftovers from the banquet sent up. A few minutes later, four men arrived in the elevator with trays. They were not allowed out onto our floor, so four of the guys went and retrieved them. We made ourselves plates of food and sat back down in front of the cozy fireplace.

Sterling ran his hand down the side of my face and then took my hand in his. "I'm sorry Eve, or I mean Enola, but I can't keep my hands off of you. You smell like cinnamon and Rosemary with a hint of vanilla. Everything that gets to me. I leaned my head on to his shoulder and breathed in the sweet smells of him. I knew we were genetically altered to have intense feelings like this and want each other so that it would ensure rapid reproduction, but it felt really nice cuddled up with him in front of a warm glowing fire in a candlelit room. His silver hair fell across my face as he leaned his head down on mine. He slipped his hand from mine and wrapped his arms around me, lifting me up and on his lap facing him. He sat forward a little and I wrapped my legs around him as our lips came together. Every part of him felt rock solid beneath me.

The kisses were gentle and the touches light. I rocked myself against him and shivered with the pleasure that ran through me. I leaned back for a better angle and moaned as he moved beneath me. He slipped my shirt over my head, and I tossed it to Haymich who was pretending not to watch us. He let out one of his roars and Sterling began licking and sucking my breast. This immediately returned my attention to the gorgeous man between my legs. I untucked his shirt and cast it aside as he moved his nuzzling to my neck and shoulders. Was I going to do this right here in front of them all? I was panting by the time he returned his mouth to mine, which I opened up eagerly to his tongue. I ran my hand through his silky, long hair and let it cascade over both of us. The muscles in my thighs were rippling with anticipation and my linen pants were drenched with need. I could feel him throbbing beneath his pants as anxious as I was to finally have penetration. I wiggled off of him and stood up, untied my linen pants, and let them fall to the floor. I heard multiple groans around the room.

I reached out my hand to Sterling; he took it and followed me to my bed. The bed was high off of the floor, so I had to crawl up on to it. Sterling pushed me flat on to my stomach and began tracing my spine with his tongue, stopping to suck here and there. I wiggled and moaned with delight. When he reached the right point, he flipped me over and began his task in front with me on the edge of the bed and him kneeling. Using his tongue, lips, and fingers he brought me to a finish quickly. I lay there throbbing and begging for more. I sat up as he was removing his pants. The rest of his amazing body did not disappoint. We began kissing and I could taste my desire on his mouth. I reached down and grabbed a hold of his and stroked it. He gently pushed me further on to the bed, climbing on top of me.

He hovered above me for a minute while we drank in each other's beauty. Then, he smiled at me as he gently entered me and threw his head back and groaned with intense pleasure. It hurt for a minute, but as he found a rhythm inside of me, I matched it as we kissed and ran our hands all over each other. I was soon on the verge of exploding again when he changed the rhythm to faster, harder, and deeper. With each thrust my pleasure built until finally it was set free and just one more thrust took care of his need. He was lying on top of me, both of us trembling and covered with sweat.

"Oh, my God! That was better than I ever imagined." I wrapped my arms tighter around him and snuggled my face into his neck. He rolled off of me, grinning from ear to ear," Give me a minute, I'm not sure we did it right so we better try again just to make sure." We both laughed. Then, I climbed on top of him. I instantly felt him react to our bodies touching. "I'm not sure you need a few minutes. Just lie there and relax, I'll do all the work this time." I moved forward and slid him back in place. Straddling his waist, I bounced and rocked on top of him, pressing my hands against his chest and throwing my head back in ecstasy. We spent the rest of the night into the early morning making sure we got it right.

Chapter Twenty-Five: The Sad Truth

Three days later, I was summoned to meet with Caesar. I actually had lost all interest in speaking with him somehow. Those three days were spent laughing, playing board games, and getting to know my new family. Of course, there was a lot of private time with Sterling and some light playful kissing and rubbing with all the others. Now I would have to put aside the fun and get back to business.

The elevator arrived, and the door opened to reveal Caesar waiting for me. We took it to the third floor and entered a large lab with many machines and large, clear, tubular vats. Caesar sat at a table next to a very stern-looking women with her hair in a tight bun and wearing a nurse's uniform. There was a chair across the table, and I sat in it without waiting to be asked. "Nurse Amber will be scanning you for medical assessment while we talk." She stood up, wrapped a cuff around my arm, and started typing into a tablet. She must have made some kind of sign to him I did not notice. "It is confirmed that you are indeed pregnant, and we are on our way to our first batch of babies. You can now have penis to vagina sex with whomever up there you want to until your next pregnancy. In two months or so, we will remove the fertilized embryos from your womb and put them in our cryogenic tanks. It will take only three more months in the tanks until they are full term. At that time, they will be removed from the tanks, evaluated, and sent to their host parents. You did well, as there are six this time. We were hoping for six to eight every three months so we are on track. So, you have five minutes to ask any of your silly questions."

He was so detached and so clinical that it was unnerving. Five minutes? I had five hundred questions. "Why can't you just clone me and the men or clone this set of babies?" I first asked. Caesar told me, "We have tried that, but genetically-created tissues cannot be cloned. Next question" Then I asked, "So, you are just going to give my babies away to those poor people out there?" Caesar told me, "Couples go through a selection process and then are set up in this facility and all of the other facilities with nice living conditions and extra rations and benefits for being a host family. They want children. No one has been able to conceive since the accident. Once your children reach puberty, we can extract their eggs and sperms to create even more babies without waiting for them to be old enough to reproduce. Time is up for now, I will see you in six weeks."

I was quickly escorted back to the top floor and nudged out of the elevator. I walked into the dining area and found Haymich sitting in a chair reading a book, Valcor eating fruit, and Phang Lee folding origami. I walked over to Haymich, "I really need one of your big bear hugs right now." He said, "I thought you might, Lass. Come sit on my lap and let me make it all better." He held open his arms for me, and I wrapped myself around his huge body, tucking my head in his neck. I felt sad I guess, feeling like this were foreign to me. I snuggled closer and felt him rise under me. "Won't be able to control that with you wiggling," he moaned. "That's okay," I replied. Then, feeling him grow even larger, I said, "That's more than okay." We began kissing while he rubbed my back, gently working his way under my shirt. When his hands contacted my skin, it was like a flare of prickly lighting ran over my entire body.

I shuddered, which made him groan and pull me into him. Haymich ran his hands up my thighs and up my skirt to my ass. "You are not wearing panties, Lass. Are you trying to kill me?" he growled in my ear. I reached between us and unbuttoned his fly, "I am pregnant," was all I had to say. He knew it meant I could have him. He reached in his pants and freed himself. Like everything else about him, it was large and hard. I grasped it with my hands and slid down onto it. We both let out a cry as he entered me. He had his hand around my ass, pushing and pulling while we grinded together. I thought we might break the chair with our frantic coupling. I bit his lip while he rubbed his thumb over my aching nipple. There together, still fully clothed, we came as one. He grabbed my face in is hands and devoured my lips. I managed to gasp out, "More." He stood up with my legs wrapped around him. I could feel him growing again inside me, and he walked us to his room. There, the clothes were removed slowly, with kisses at each new naked place. He made it all better as promised, over and over again.d

Chapter Twenty-Six: Six Weeks

My men were very attentive toward me and barely acknowledge the existence of Zaynep and Robyn. Sometimes, they both slept in my gigantic bed with me and whichever of my lovely harem spent the night. Occasionally, one or both of the girls would spend the night with one of the other companions. And, once in a while, a companion would stay the night in one of the men's rooms. Usually they just came up to our floor to hang out, play cards, or have little quickies. So far, I had not invited anyone to join any of us in sexual activity. I liked multiple partners like Zaynep and Graven had introduced me to, but the one on one personal attention I was getting from my men, all but Ollaff, was special. So far Ollaff had remained aloof; once in a while he has let me kiss him but then he shies away.

Djorg entered my bedroom, carrying a tray of fresh fruits, pastries, and juice. He has spent all night with me and snuck out early to prepare us breakfast in bed. He set the tray on the table next to the bed and climbed back in with me. "I thought that with all the activity last night, you must be starving. But you look very edible yourself this morning." I was naked and looking at the slight swell of my belly while lying in the middle of the bed. He crawled over to me like a great black panther on the prowl. His Mahogany skin was such a contrast to my almost translucent skin. He kissed my forehead, lips, neck, and breasts, and he worked his way down between my legs. I gladly opened up to him, already moist with anticipation. I ran my hands over his bald head and shoulders as he worked magic with his tongue.

Robyn walked through the door just as I was begging for more. She turned to leave, "So sorry, I thought you were eating. I'll come back later." "Are you not interested in maybe joining us for a minute?" I looked down at Djorn, who did not miss a lick and only nodded in agreement. Robyn had her hair down today, a flame cascading down her back. She took a few steps closer, "Are you sure? I'd love to!" I nodded and she quickly removed her dress, where she was naked beneath it. Robyn climbed in to the bed and looked unsure as to what to do. I motioned her to lie by me, and she complied. "Kiss me," I whispered to her, as I wiggled from the exquisite pleasure between my legs. She leaned over me, and we began kissing, I found her breast and began playing with the nipples.

I had never touched such large breasts, and they excited me even more. Very quickly, Djorg finished his quest and crawled up to join us. I took Robyn's hand and led it to the need in him. Together we rubbed and caressed him while still kissing each other. He moaned, pulled us apart, and straddled me. He slid into me while pulling Robyn on top of me facing him. They began to kiss while he rocked inside me. I had my hands on Robyn's back and ass, kneading and rubbing as my pleasure built again. Djorg suckled her breasts while he plunged his fingers in her, causing her to cry out and throw her arms around him. I could feel him inside me and I could also feel his finger working her as she dripped her pleasure on my belly. She suddenly sagged into him, panting and laughing. He slid her to lie beside us and began violently thrusting and grunting like the wild beast he is. Only a few moments later, all three of us lay on the bed, panting, sweating, and glowing with fulfillment. Maybe extra people are not a bad thing after all.

The fact that Ollaff seemed to not want me was on my mind all the time. What would happen when it was his turn to impregnate me? All of us were bisexual by nature, but I felt that maybe he had never been allowed to play with women at all and preferred the attentions of other men. I decided to have a heart to heart conversation with him, after I showered of course. I excused myself from my bed where we had been nibbling on the fruit after our threesome and headed to get cleaned up. Robyn was waiting for me with a towel and robe as I opened the shower door. She was still flush and her pale skin made it stand out. For once, she was not chattering away a million miles an hour. We did not discuss our interlude at all but got right to drying my hair. It was strange to have someone always there helping me with normal daily activities, but I could get used to it.

Dried and dressed, I left my quarters. I did not let Robyn do anything with my hair today except brush it. I was wearing a long, flowing skirt that was a deep burgundy with a gold inlay. My top was barely there. It was made of silk and the same burgundy shade as the skirt. In the light, you could see right through it. I was on a mission to find Ollaff and seduce him. I presumed I would need assistance, and I had already decided to ask Caspian. I was in luck, as they were both in the main room. "Caspian, Ollaff, may I speak to both of you privately? In my room." They both stood up and followed me, though Ollaff did it rather reluctantly. I decided not to lead them to the bed, but instead, I asked them to sit on the pillows and fluffy carpet under the window. I stood in the sunlight to make sure they could both see my naked breasts beneath the clinging silk. "I'd like to ask you a favor, both of you. I would like to have sex with all three of us together. Ollaff is not comfortable with me alone, and I think if you were here, Caspian, he would allow me to touch him. Are you both willing?"

Caspian gave me a sexy smile, "I'll show him the ropes. What do you say Ollaff?" Ollaff did not answer; he just took off his shirt and laid back on the pillows. "You will need to take off more than that." Caspian said as he slowly ran his hand down Ollaff's chest and under his pants. Ollaff closed his eyes and smiled. "He may be shy everywhere but down here." Caspian giggled. I got on the other side of Ollaff and did the same thing, except I kissed my way down. By the time I got to his waist, his pants were pulled low on his thighs and he was free. I wasted no time playing and I took all of him in my mouth. I felt him shudder and heard him gasp. Caspian removed his own clothes, moved behind me, and slid himself gently inside me. I groaned with my mouth full, and that seemed to excite Ollaff even more. He began thrusting his hips and pulled my head down further into him. I felt his warmth deep in my throat as he cried out my name. I continued to stroke him while Caspian finished, too. Ollaff still had some life in him so Caspian and I pulled his pants all the way off. Ollaff sat up and I sat down on him. He was so large in the waist and thighs that I had trouble creating much movement.

Caspian knelt behind me, grabbed me by my waist, and moved my body in slow up and down, back and forth movements as he kissed my neck and back. In between panting and groaning, Olaff sucked on my breasts. He grabbed my face in his large strong hands and looked me in the eyes. "Don't stop, Enola!" He pulled my face closer and kissed me frantically while he bucked beneath me. The three of us lie there on the pillows, basking in the sun and the warmth of making love. "I am sorry I avoided this Eve. . Enola. I was not sure if I would react the same to a woman or if it would satisfy me. Now I don't know how I will keep my hands off of you." "Well, that is the good part my love," I said. "You don't have to, and I don't want you to." A week later, Ollaff proved himself quite capable of being pleasde by and pleasing women. He spent all night in bed with Zaynep, Robyn, and I.

Chapter Twenty-Seven: WTF

We were all gathered in the living room doing various things. I was curled up with the dog on my lap, drawing Phang Lee's profile with a pencil in my sketch book. He was sitting across from me just gazing into the fire. Z was stretched out on the floor, looking very Cleopatra-ish, as she played a board game with Robyn, Casper, Haymitch, and Valcor. Djorn and Haymitch were animatedly discussing battle techniques, while Olaff watched attentively and interjected his opinions on occasion. Raven Wing was standing behind me, combing my hair and telling me an old Indian fable about a turtle. Sterling was reading a book, sitting between my legs with one arm wrapped around my thigh.

It was a perfectly normal afternoon, we had just finished lunch and we were relaxing together as usual. In the past nineteen months, we had settled into a family routine and were all very content. I had produced a "litter" from each one of my men, and now Caesar did not hold me to being with just one of them at a time. We had given life to 7seventy-eight healthy children so far, and I was currently carrying seven. I looked down at Sterling's long, silver hair between my legs and a shiver of passion went through me. We have all found our groove in our strange family and have eased into a very satisfying habit of pleasing each other. I normally engaged in sex with all of them every day in some way, shape, or form. Most of the time, there were two or three engaged in the activity with me at the same time, but they all also got their private moments.

Djorg was partial to group affairs, as were Caspian, Olaff, and Phang Lee. They liked all the other men and the girls to be involved. Raven Wing was almost exclusively a private session, but he would get a little involved if we happened to get into some playful slap and tickle outside of the bedroom. Valcor, Sterling, and Haymitch liked for Zeynep and Robyn to join in, and they would watch me with other men, but those three preferred not to get touchy feely with men themselves. There was a lot of physical contact twenty-four hours a day. I could not walk by any of them without a touch or kiss, which the majority of the time led to more.

It was absolute bliss until the day my mother showed up in the Tower. I was sent a message from the council that she had been located in another facility and was now here, in the lower housing area. I had not seen my parents in nine years, and I was thrilled to learn that my mother was alive and here where I could see her. I was not allowed to leave our penthouse floor without an escort from Caesar or his designated men. I called down to his office, over the top excited, and he would not speak to me. His secretary informed me that he was in meetings with key persons who had just arrived and none of them would be available for personal conversations until further notice. I was devastated to say the least. Wouldn't my mother be demanding to see me like I was for her? Where was my father? So many questions now assaulted my mind, and I had no way to get answers until they allowed me to.

When I was first brought up to the penthouse and told that I was not allowed to leave, I was very upset about it. I felt like a prisoner, but all of the boys told me that they had felt the same way at first, too. They came to realize that it was safer and healthier to remain there and that everything they need was provided as promised. It did not take me long to adopt the same attitude and begin enjoying our life without a thought about being confined against my will. Now, with the arrival of my mother, all those feeling resurfaced.

I was staring at the intercom when Valcor walked in to check on me. I ran into his arms and began rambling about being kept from seeing my mom. He hugged me tight, stroked my hair, and quietly listened to me. As I calmed down, the gentle stroking became more caressing and we began to kiss. I let myself go to the passion and unbuttoned his pants. I slid them over his slim waist, and he stepped out of them as they hit the floor. He usually wanted a lot of foreplay and I usually accommodated him on that. This time, however, I wanted him quickly and violently. He knew me well enough to know how I was feeling and what I needed, so he yanked my flowered sundress over my head and tossed it across the room. Valcor pressed me up against the wall as we fondled each other and tried to explore each other's tonsils with our tongues. He lifted me up, and I wrapped my legs around him as he slammed me into the wall. It took a minute to guide his huge erection to the proper angle to enter me, but I got it in. His head arched back as he entered me, and we both made enough noise that gathered the crowd from the next room. With each thrust, I was slammed into the wall and cried out with pleasure. It was over for us both in a matter of minutes.

I settled down on the floor, surrounded by my new family and told them about my mother being in the Tower and how they were not letting me see her right away. Everyone reassured me that they would reunite us soon. Maybe my mother needed rest, medical attention, or something else before such an emotional event. They were sure to be keeping her best interest at heart. There was no telling what my mother had been through.

Chapter Twenty-Eight: Mom

The next day, I paced around our living quarters all morning, running scenarios over in my head and bouncing ideas off of my lovers. When the intercom alerted, I ran to it, vibrating with excitement. Enry, one of Cesar's guards, informed me that he was on his way up to escort me to a meeting. He clicked off without any further information. I kissed and hugged each one of my family members and skipped out the door, down the hallway to the elevator. Moments later, Enry arrived and I entered the elevator brimming with joy. His demeanor did not match mine. As always, he was stoic and militant, looking forward, back straight, and not even a hint of emotion. I raised up on my tiptoes and gave him a quick kiss on the cheek. He had no reaction, as always. It made we wonder if he was a genetically-altered human as well, made to be a good little robot.

The elevator quickly reached the ground floor. This was the level that held conference rooms and lower level labs. I did not expect this to be the floor he took me to. My mother would surely have an apartment on a higher level, and her working lab would also would be on the highest level. This floor was for meetings of the council and for banquets. Maybe they are giving my mother a welcoming reception. I wish I had been informed if this is the case, as I would have dressed better. As the door opened, I hopped out and immediately looked around, only to discover that there was no one, literally no one, around. I turned back toward the open elevator doors as Enry stepped out, briskly turned right and walked down the hall toward the council conference room. I assumed I was expected to follow him and did so with a slight hesitation. Something was not right about this. He led me to the door, and he also seemed hesitant to open it. This was the first time he had ever seemed human to me. His hesitation added to my apprehension.

I entered the room to find the entire councik waiting for me. My mother, however, was nowhere in sight. I did not approach the stage where their chairs were set up like judges presiding over a court room. My hesitation seemed to make Caesar smirk. "Come closer and stop wasting our time girl," he hissed. "You and your companions have been living a dream, free to do as you wish and live a life of luxury. The time has come that we, the council, have made the decision that our original plans for you would be less costly to us. We have never needed your cooperation to get what we needed from you, it just seemed more humane at the time. The majority of the low caste people have forgotten about you and none of them actually ever cared what was happening in regard to you anyway. Instead of letting you frolic and get pregnant, we will now put you in a cryo tube of suspended animation and let the computer system impregnate you and harvest the embryos on a rigid schedule. Your body systems will be stimulated by the computer, and it will ensure that everything you need to produce what we want is provided to your body. All these years we were just waiting for the genetic scientists and computer specialists to perfect the system and now they finally have."

Caesar continued, "The woman you have been demanding to see and that you obviously still believe to be your actual mother has come to sedate you, place you in a chemically-induced coma and accompany you to the facility that houses the Life Systems. Keep in mind, I did not have to tell you any of this, but the council agreed that it would be the right thing to do." Before he had even finished his last sentence, my mother quickly approached me from behind Enry. "Hold her," she said as she plunged a needle in to my neck and released its contents into my jugular vein. I did not even have the time to gasp. Everything went black as I felt Enry lift me up like a sleeping child and carry me away.

Chapter Thirty: Life Systems Facility

Nanette entered the Life Systems Facility with lots of apprehension. It was her first day at the new job and only her second day in the Canopy Facility. She had been recruited from the underground facility in Connecticut where she had been in an advanced computer program for six years. Now, she would be working in the most prestigious lab on New Earth. At the ripe age of sixteen, it was a great honor. Her parents were on the original council at the main facility and were very proud of her. She had very pale, luminescent skin and long, ebony hair that really brought out her purple cat-like eyes. She is tall for her age and possesses a very athletic build. She achieved her first college degree at ten years old and her doctorate at fourteen. She was vibrating with anticipation and walked to the security desk with her head held high and her shoulders back.

The scientist she was replacing at the facility, Christine, was waiting there to greet her and show her around. "Hello and welcome. My name is Christine. I have been anxious for your arrival. Three years here is long enough, and I can't wait to turn it all over to you so that I can move on." Christine handed her a syringe that contained a Nano byte system that she needed to inject in her arm. Once injected, all the doors would automatically unlock as she approached, and she would have complete access to most of the computer systems. Nanette injected the Nano bytes and returned the used syringe to Christine. "Let's get started then," she said with her signature toothy grin.

The facility was not very large. In fact, it was much smaller than Nanette had imagined it would be. There were only store rooms on the first floor and her office and living quarters on the second floor. The third floor housed the security staff and maintenance. The top floor was the computer system and the cryo vault. After a brief tour of her office and living quarters, the two ladies took the elevator the computer systems room. This would be where Nanette would be spending the majority of her time for the next three years, just as Christine had done.

"The entire system runs itself," Christine explained. "We are only assigned her in case something goes wrong. Nothing ever has, at least to my knowledge. I have been bored to death. As you probably also think, I thought being involved in such a complex advanced system would be fun and educational. It isn't." She pointed out all of the monitors and system checks that needed to be completed twice a day then led Nanette into the vault. The vault was a large glass tube filled with an embryotic type fluid. Inside the tube was a woman. She had tubes coming out of her mouth, stomach, urethra, and anus. There were probes attached to her that led to a bod at the end of the tube.

She appeared to be in her twenties, pale and thin with crazy red curly hair. You could see tiny ripples in the fluid as the probes stimulated her muscles and nerves to keep her body in top physical condition. There were tubes surgically implanted by her hips that went to her ovaries. The scene took Nanette back a little. "I knew there was a genetically created humanoid that they used for research here, but I did not expect this. I am not sure what I expected. How long has she been in there?" Christine shrugged her shoulders, "As far as I have been told, she has always been in there. She was created in there and will always be there. They stimulate her brain so I assume she has thoughts, and you will see that she does dream, which I found creepy. What could she dream about? She has never been alive to have experiences."

Nanette noticed a word written on the tank in front the humanoids' face. She stepped closer and read it out loud, "Alone. What does that mean?" she asked. "I don't know, someone wrote that on there before I got here. Stupid thing is if she could see it, it would be backwards, ENOLA. That isn't even a word, not that she will ever see it." Neither girl noticed that the humanoid opened her eyes for a brief moment before they sleepily shut again.

The girls spent the even chatting and getting Nanette settled in. Christine left first thing in the morning when the escorts came to take her back for debriefing and to give her a new assignment. Nanette grabbed her laptop, filled with old black and white movies and several from the 1980s, and headed up to the computer center. "This is going to be a long three years," she said to herself as she stepped out of the elevator. "At least it is not as long as long as that poor creature has been held in the tank."